3

WB 15

BUZZARD POINT

After a street shooting in a Texas cow town, Jesse Tripp is forced to flee his family home. Two years later, he makes a reluctant return and finds his father dead and his brother Owen in control of the family's Triple T ranch. Suddenly, Jesse needs to consider his situation. Taking to the hills again isn't an option, so should he fight to retain what's rightfully his? Sparks will fly before the dust settles on the Triple T ranch . . .

Books by Caleb Rand
in the Linford Western Library:

THE EVIL STAR
WOLF MEAT
YELLOW DOG
COLD GUNS
THE GOOSE MOON
THE ROSADO GANG
LIZARD WELLS
WILD MEDDOW

CALEB RAND

BUZZARD POINT

Complete and Unabridged

LINFORD
Leicester

First published in Great Britain in 2011 by
Robert Hale Limited
London

First Linford Edition
published 2012
by arrangement with
Robert Hale Limited
London

British Library CIP Data

Rand, Caleb.
    Buzzard Point.- -(Linford western library)
    1. Western stories.
    2. Large type books.
    I. Title II. Series
    823.9'2–dc23

    ISBN 978–1–4448–1169–8

Published by
F. A. Thorpe (Publishing)
Anstey, Leicestershire

Set by Words & Graphics Ltd.
Anstey, Leicestershire
Printed and bound in Great Britain by
T. J. International Ltd., Padstow, Cornwall

This book is printed on acid-free paper

1

One hundred miles south of the Texas-New Mexico border, it was nearing first dark as the empty cattle train ground its way from the stockyards of Chimney Point.

A hundred yards behind the brake wagon, light rain fell across Jesse Tripp's back as he ran across the acrid, hard-packed dirt. He was naked to the waist, held his hat on his head with one hand, juggled his shirt, jacket, boots and gun rig with the other. In his panicky haste, his legs were buckling, but he guessed he could make it to the slow-moving cars.

Behind him he heard a shot and then an overhead whine. He knew if he looked around he'd see an enraged man clutching a big Colt, shooting as he ran, panting and blowing in single-minded pursuit. A couple of bullets went wide, but two more got close, struck sparks from the couplings on a stock wagon.

Stumbling in his stride, Jesse strained to catch up with the train. His legs pounded, and the breath rasped at the back of his throat as he cursed. Alongside him he saw movement within the shadowy interior of a bull wagon, then two men appeared. They grinned and yelled encouragement, offered their hands as he closed in.

'Don't worry. There ain't no bulls in here 'cept us, feller,' one of them yelled. 'Toss up your stuff.'

But Jesse Tripp had lost belongings that way before. He pictured the deceiving hands suddenly disappearing, the door sliding to with a bang, closing him out. Then another bullet struck the side of the car. He cursed again, jerked his body into a final effort and flung up his bundle. He wondered if he would have to shoot anyone and hung on to his gun rig. But he reached up, found a safe grip in their outstretched hands. He hurled himself into the car, brought his laughing helpers down in a heap as they fell backwards. He thought he heard one more shot, and he dragged himself back to the edge of the doorway and looked out.

The man who was now running around the stock pens slipped. He lifted his Colt once more, but the hammer fell on an empty chamber. Exhausted and angry he fell to his knees, beat his thigh with the frame of his gun.

Jesse grinned thankfully as he moved back into the car. The rain was still glistening on his upper body as he looked around at his fellow travellers.

'Come home early, did he?' asked a scruffy youngster with pimples and a grin that half split his face.

'Reckon,' Jesse replied after a slight hesitation. 'I wasn't goin' to stay an' ask either of 'em.'

'Nothin' quite like the flavour o' forbidden fruit,' scoffed a hairy-faced man with a thick neck.

'Huh, ain't that the truth,' Jesse said, sitting up and rubbing his chest with his jacket. Then he pulled on his shirt and stood, buckling on the gunbelt. 'I'm just thankful you're all goin' not comin'. Accommodation shared with a breed bull ain't my idea o' ridin' first class.'

They laughed again and shared brief introductions. The one with the beard was Buffler. The youngest and smallest of the trio was Pollo. The third man was a quiet fair-head, who said he was called Orm. To Jesse they were obvious and fitting travelling names, and what they wished to call themselves didn't matter. The men had been paid off after driving a herd in from Mexico. They had also sold their ponies, were trying to save the dollars they had made by riding an empty car back home.

Jesse stood six foot in his boots, was slim from top to bottom. The others were quick to notice he was also tough, had recovered quickly after his run to catch the train. He looked like a man who was comfortable with himself, possessed character that was reflected in his watchful blue eyes. A lock of black hair that curled across his forehead, gave him a younger look than his thirty years.

Pollo handed him the makings, and Jesse shook his head. 'Stunts your growth,' he said without sounding personal.

'Where you headed?' the youngster asked, uncertain of the dig.

Jesse shrugged. 'Where the trail ends, same as always,' he said. 'El Paso, Van Horn, maybe somewhere along the way. Don't matter much. I ain't got kin quarters.'

'Yeah, just use other people's,' the youngster smirked, jerked a thumb back down the track.

Jesse smiled thinly, and then there was silence. If the men were waiting for him to respond in some way, they were out of luck.

'Well, I got a pack o' cards,' Pollo said. 'If we got a way to go, what about a friendly hand o' somethin'?'

'I ain't got more'n a couple o'

dollars,' Jesse replied.

'Hell, none of us got much more'n that,' Buffler growled and wiped his big hands on the seat of his pants. 'Deal 'em, kid. Let's put some pennies into circulation. Perhaps my luck's changed since last night.' The heavy-set man glanced at Jesse. 'Lost me a bundle in a goddamn dog hole they was callin' an 'otel. They set me up,' he added, by way of defence. 'Let me win a few hands till I thought I was wallowin' in the plush, then they came at me. Goddamn tinhorns. Lucky I ain't taken a dip since Christmas last, else they'd have taken my shirt.'

★   ★   ★

Pollo snorted indifferently and rolled out a wellworn horse blanket. The men spread it across the dirt-crusted boards of the bull pen and they started to play five-card stud. Jesse sat in for the first few hands just to get an idea of his opponents. But turning down the first two cards of every hand wasn't a safe procedure with strangers. No player liked being sized-up by someone who wasn't slipping money into the pot. It was obvious Buffler was an intolerant, reckless player. He was trying to make good each loss by doubling up on the next hand, no matter what cards he held. Orm played his own game, calm and cautious. Pollo fumbled around with the careless enthusiasm of youth.

Jesse reckoned he could likely win himself a few dollars before one of the sharpers decided to slit his throat. The Pecos trestle bridge was a likely spot for a sooner than expected departure from the train, let alone the world of the living.

When the next game started and Buffler dealt him his two cards, the up card was the three of hearts. With his hand screening his hole card he took an impassive look to see the four of spades. He was travelling hopefully in more ways than one, so he was up for a fifty cent bet when it came his turn. Orm had the highest up-card, but he opened with a dollar after a close study of his holer. With his face barely able to control his excitement, Pollo covered. It seemed obvious to Jesse that the youngster was starting with a pair, held something that matched his nine of diamonds up-card.

When Buffler covered too, it left Jesse with no choice if he wanted to continue. Although he had already lost more than he had intended, his next dealt card was the two of clubs; the making of a small straight. Orm was dealt the highest up-card so he bet again, with another dollar. Impatiently, Buffler snarled at Pollo to follow; he hesitated just long enough to extend his grin, before covering the bet and raising it by fifty cents.

Although Jesse looked cool on the surface, he could feel the heat breaking across his chest. For a man with next to nothing, the scale of betting was already way above small peas. By goading Pollo, Buffler was starting a harrying tactic.

They wanted to get hold of what little he had quickly, and Jesse wondered how long before the train made it to the bridge.

There was, however, one way he could stall and he took it. When his turn came, he checked his hole card again. 'I'll stick with these,' he offered.

He could see by their faces that the others didn't like it much, but Jesse didn't like being crowded. Buffler flicked his next card at him face up, Jesse's mouth tightened slowly when he saw it was the six of spades. If he could manage to stay in the game long enough for the next deal, he'd be looking out for any one of four cards.

Jesse let his breath hiss out slowly as he was dealt the five of diamonds as his final card. But Buffler knew that Jesse didn't have enough cash to see out the round of bets and he smiled crookedly.

Orm's face gave nothing away. The very best he could have from the look of his cards was a pair of kings, but it would beat the nines that Pollo was showing. Jesse guessed that Orm would go on for a few rounds just by bluffing, and Pollo would panic after a couple more rounds and probably fold. It would be Buffler who would stay. His dark eyes were already flicking with excitement at the prospect of holding the winning hand.

Jesse pushed his remaining stake into the centre when his turn came and Buffler raised it.

'This should see you off, fancy man,' he said, and sniffed smugly.

2

Jesse blinked, shook his head as the train rolled on. He looked out through the partly open door, but not realizing that so much time had gone by, was surprised to see that first dark was already crowding in. The locomotive whistled as they neared a bend on a grade, then slowed as the track began to wind through a range of hills. They were edging the Pecos River on the edge of the Edwards Plateau, and the car rocked and clacked over the joints in the tracks.

'Looks like the night might win this game,' he said. He shivered, pulled on his jacket and buttoned it up. Then he eased back and calmly brought out his Colt.

The three other men stiffened as Jesse hefted the gun in the palm of his hand. But he smiled and laid it on the floor. 'It's a .36 Navy Colt that they probably don't make the like of no more. It must be worth a few dollars, gentlemen. I'll take five for it on this hand, an' five on the next,' he suggested. 'What do you say?'

But the men weren't set to accept anything that Jesse put to them, especially Buffler.

'We got ourselves strictly cash stakes, mister,' the man said. 'So either you find some or shut up.'

Jesse's jaw twitched and his eyes narrowed slightly. 'Where this train's headed, a fine smoke pole like this could be the difference 'tween livin' or dyin'. Maybe I'll be doin' one o' you a real favour,' he replied.

'Yeah, maybe, but like I said, we bet ready money,' Buffler insisted.

'Ah come on, Buffler, what the hell's it matter?' Orm said. 'It ain't like we're takin' on the Golden Nugget.'

'I already got me a gun,' Buffler growled.

'Then sell it,' Jesse advised. 'If you win, that is.'

'Huh, come on, Buffler. Gun's got to be worth at least ten dollars,' Pollo said.

'Aaaagh, then just to shut you up,' Buffler growled. 'For this hand only.'

'I only got the one gun,' Jesse informed them. 'I'm goin' to be flushed or finished.'

Buffler looked at Orm. 'Are you raisin' or foldin'?' he snapped.

Jesse grinned with satisfaction. 'Sittin' on somethin' pretty good?' he queried.

'You'll find out soon enough,' Buffler gruffed. 'Get on with it, Orm,' he persisted.

Buffler already had a pair of queens showing in front of him, and Orm thought he must be sitting on three of a kind. Orm took another look at Buffler's card, but his nerve broke and he folded. Likewise, Pollo whistled air between his lips, shook his head and turned his cards in. Buffler smirked and pushed all his money into the pile.

'Well, Mister fancy-gun man, I reckon I'll just call your bluff,' he challenged. The man was so intent on winning the hand, he didn't even consider raising the bet any further.

'So let's take a look at that holer o' yours,' Jesse said.

Buffler shook his head. 'You know I don't have to do that. There's some sort o' gambit that says it's what *you* got that counts.'

Jesse kept his face blank as he fanned out his cards. 'Yeah, sorry. For a moment there, I weren't sure we had any o' them,' he muttered, made a wry smile. Then he flipped over his hole card and dropped it on top of the others. 'Say hello to Buffler,' he said.

Orm swallowed, shook his head and Pollo snorted.

Buffler's face drained, and one of his eyelids twitched as he stared at Jesse. 'You been sittin' on that four all along?' he asked.

'The only thing I been sittin' on's dried bullshit,' Jesse rasped back. 'An' there's nothin' against that.' Jesse holstered his Colt and raked in his winnings. 'Besides, I ain't that much of a player to go riskin' my gun on nothin'.'

Buffler's face turned ugly, twitched first then hardened. 'You shouldn't have bet with that goddamn sixgun,' he gritted. 'The hand should've been mine.'

'If you hadn't had them dollars, I'd probably have let you use a pistol for collateral,' Jesse obliged.

Pollo eased back a little, but Orm laid a hand on Buffler's thick arm. 'Yeah, ease up. Buffler,' he suggested uneasily. 'We all agreed.'

Buffler was pondering on the gist of Jesse's slight. 'Don't mean to say it was right,' he growled.

Jesse smiled drily. 'Sometimes you live on the difference between right an' wrong. I thought you'd have known that,' he said. 'I'm willin' to play on, if you want.'

'An' what am I supposed to play with?' Buffler demanded pointing to the winnings now stacked in front of Jesse. 'You just took my last red cent.' He leaned on the knuckles of a big fist, thrust his face in close. 'You want I should put up *my* pistol?'

Jesse fixed him with a steady gaze. 'As long as it matches the stake, you can put up whatever you want. What you're totin', looks like it might have some antique value.'

Pollo grinned. 'That's fair enough, Buffler. Let's play some more,' he suggested with a nervy laugh.

'Shut it, kid,' Buffler snorted back.

But Jesse knew that Buffler didn't want to carry on. The man wanted a fight because he'd guessed wrong, been made to look foolish in front of his fellow travellers.

'You insult my piece, you insult *me*,' he said with contrived menace. 'An' I ain't got to know you well enough to let it rest there.' He grunted once, then going with a lurch of the car, he lunged forward.

Jesse threw himself backwards as a heavy fist flailed the air. Money spilled across the floor, as he scrambled up fast. Buffler caught him on the point of the shoulder, and he rolled into a corner, cursed and spat as he got to his knees. Damn trouble, he thought and cursed again. It was dogging him, had already driven him from his home town, and now, without any invitation it was back.

He ducked another balled fist, sunk a blow into Buffler's thick middle as the man charged in again.

Jesse raised himself to his feet to meet Buffler's head on charge, resolutely held his ground against the rock and sway of the floor. He took a couple of hard blows to his head and body, then he gritted his teeth and ripped two punches into Buffler's face. It brought the man up short, and Jesse stepped in, stomped hard with his heel on to the man's instep. Buffler howled and doubled over and Jesse brought a knee up into the front of his face. The man half straightened before crashing back against a wall of the car. His nose was broken and blood was smeared across his face.

'Hey, that's enough,' Orm yelled and went for Jesse.

Jesse was caught by surprise and took a flurry of wild punches that sent him back down on one knee. As he dodged a kick, he grabbed out at Orm's boot, held it and twisted. The man shouted and spun across the car, falling halfway out the door. Wanting no part in the fight, Pollo pressed himself back against the wall, bug-eyed and pale.

Jesse staggered up, stumbled forward as Orm slid past his point of balance. Orm yelled for Buffler, but the man wasn't going to help. He shook his bloody head, as he pushed himself away from the wall.

Jesse made a grab for Orm's sweaty jacket, started to heave the man back in. 'Goddamnit, you're supposed to be the quiet one,' he rasped.

'He's still one of us,' Orm coughed out, as Jesse dragged him back into the car.

Then, a knee slammed into Jesse's kidneys, and nausea flooded through him. He caught another blow in the middle of his back and felt himself lurch from the boxcar. Smoke and cinders blew into his face, a gust of fresh rain, then he glimpsed sparks flying from the loco's smokestack. The engine was lumbering around a bend, and far below, at the foot of a steep slope, water gleamed like a silver ribbon in the dark.

As he fell, he caught a short, cruel laugh from Buffler, and then he was falling free into the rainlashed night. He landed flat on his back, jerked and rolled. Above him, he momentarily saw a red blur that was the train's tail lamp, and then there came a massive bone-jarring thud that smashed consciousness from him. He ricocheted through the rocks, his body slewing then jolting down the steep slope. Finally, he crashed through a tangle of mesquite, came to rest in the rock-strewn shallows of the Pecos.

3

The icy water churned around Jesse, and within moments he shook violently as the chill bit deep into his body. But he forced himself to his hands and knees, crawled back to the bank to collapse in the mesquite that had broken his fall.

It was full dark before he moved again. He shook his head, but it was a mistake. His brain felt like it had broken loose and he grimaced as pain spiked down his neck into his spine and lower back. He pressed his temples into the palms of his thorn-scarred hands, cursed quietly at the thought of Buffler's boot. He slowly raised his eyes, saw that the rain had stopped, was probably starting its climb up and over the second range. Then he saw some irregular, colourless shapes up the slope and he tensed, squinted uneasily for a while before realizing it was his hat and jacket caught up in a thicket near the tracks. He suffered a long involuntary shiver in his wet clothes, figured that Pollo, or more likely Orm had tossed them from the train after him. He shrugged gratefully into the heavy denim, buttoned it tight across his chest and checked his gun. He gritted his jaw to stop his teeth chattering, then kicked and dragged out a shelter under a shrubby tree. 'Ain't no Alhambra,' he mumbled with a grimace. 'Cheaper though.'

* * *

With morning, Jesse was bone tired and stiff and his face was sore. He held his arms across his chest, and lay very quiet until the sun's early rays brought the feeling of warmth. Then he made his way carefully down through the mesquite slope to the river, where he had a drink and washed his face. For a few moments he stared thoughtfully at the swirling current, then he wished he had something to eat and started off downstream.

There was one freight train and one stock train a week to Van Horn and El Paso, so there was no point in waiting for one to come by. And he didn't aim to go back upstream, where the Pecos ran close to the town he'd left in such a hurry.

Jesse knew roughly where he was out of Chimney Point, but wasn't sure how far it was to the next town west. He knew the Sierra Blanca Mountains, knew that if he made the climb on a clear day, he'd probably be able to see his home town. When he'd left Wickett, two years ago, it was the Blancas that had helped him shake off the men who were pursuing him. But he wasn't getting within long spitting distance of what was in wait for him back there.

For the remainder of the day, Jesse followed the Pecos south through wild, desolate country. Just after first dark he shot a jack-rabbit, stuffed it with a few wild onions and roasted it over a small fire. He filled his belly with clean water but remained hungry. 'If I wanted to live off goddamn mesquite beans, I'd have stayed where I was,' he mused drily.

The following noon, he paused in a small canyon where the river gathered speed. He lay in the swift flowing current, felt the cold water embrace his aching limbs. He stayed until the sharp chill started to find its way inside him, then shaking water from his ears, tried to identify the noise he was picking up. From behind a line of distant timber that ran between the hills, he heard the unmistakable sounds of a cattle herd. Upstream, the river meandered away from stands of ash and juniper, but if there was pasture beyond, maybe a ranch wouldn't be too far away. He quickly got dressed, bashed his hat back into shape and dragged on his boots.

Having worked his way through

wandering old moss horns and a few scatterlings, he came across it just before full dark. He followed the drifting trail of woodsmoke over a low rise to where the rudimentary cabin nestled. The planked door was shut and there was a dull glow from a dusted single window; a crooked stovepipe shoved its way through a sod roof that had turned wild. A pair of man's longjohns and a woman's homespun petticoat hung from a wash-line, and Jesse cracked a thin smile. Then he grimaced at the pungent bite of sizzling lard, and his belly grumbled with hunger.

Half-a-dozen horses stood together. They were quietly puffing the ground in the pole corral, but it was the saddle draped over the top rail of the fence by the gate that brought a grunt of approval from Jesse.

The underside of the rig was warm when he slipped it off the rail, and he figured the rancher had only just returned for his supper. He wanted a mount with a turn of pace, knew he was taking a chance. 'Which o' you jug heads won't be run down by the others?' he muttered, and selected a claybank mare, within five minutes had it under the saddle. Jesse knew that small-time ranchers were usually the most persistent in trying to recover property stolen from them. They had too little of just about everything and couldn't afford to lose any of it. He was mindful that they were also mostly tough and dogged, when a rifle shot crashed out from the cabin.

'Get away from my horses,' a man dressed in frayed work clothing yelled and fired again.

Jesse cursed, and skidded the horse around a tumbledown barn, across the low picket of a chicken coop. The birds squawked and fluttered with fright. The horse snorted and pounded on through a vegetable patch before Jesse could swerve it aside. Then the irate rancher was around the barn, his rifle cracking out again.

'Nellie. Saddle up the biter,' the man shouted back to his wife. 'We've got ourselves a goddamn horse-thief.'

Jesse repeated his cursing as another bullet whined overhead, then he was mounted and kicking into the home pasture, heading for the timberline. desperately. It was no use riding back to the river, there was too much open country to cross. Furthermore, an early moon was now showing big and full.

If he couldn't lose the man in the trees he would have to swing into open country towards the salt lakes. 'Goddamn dirt farmer thinks I'm for real . . . sounds like he wants me dead,' he rasped. As a last resort, he could ride on to New Mexico, realized that either way he was being forced towards home territory, almost to the outskirts of Wickett. Whether he liked it or not, he was caught between a hard place and a big rock.

As a fix, he could stand and shoot it out with the rancher who was chasing him, kill him more than likely. He wished the man no harm, but, for the loan of a horse and saddle, he wasn't going to be forced back to a place he'd vowed never, ever to return. He cursed aloud, asked why the hell the man chasing him, didn't know that. But, wanting to avoid a shoot out and riding the rancher's best mount, he'd been forced deeper into a part of that range he hadn't wanted to go. Already, he was into lost canyon country, where there was no water and little chance of food. The only way out was up and over, across the border.

And now, thoughtfully sitting the claybank on top of a ridge, he looked out across the prairie to where a reddish bluff rose from the plains and the town of Wickett. He could skirt around the scattered, low-lying buildings of course, like the smart river did, but every other direction held a threat. South was ranch country, with his father's land close-bordering the trail he'd be taking. North were law officers anxious to lay hands on him, and somewhere not far to the east, the pursuing rancher was still tracking his claybank. Yeah, he thought. It was a *few* hard places and more than *one* big rock.

4

Jesse sighed resignedly and started the claybank down from the ridge. Figuring it was the proverbial red road — the one with more hope — he figured he might as well go see how the old place and its folk were faring, if a couple of years had made them any more amenable.

Approaching the town, Jesse realized there were a few people he would actually want to see again. His pa and Owen were never far from his thoughts, as was Lupin Contento, the young Mexican girl who'd worked on the ranch. There were certainly some good times in the mix, and now he was hoping the bad ones had been forgiven or forgotten — like the death of Billy Hugh.

Jesse turned in the saddle and looked back across the flats towards the distant ranges, but there was no sign of a rider. All good chases eventually come to an end, he thought. Anyway, he was now at the edge of town, and he gave the claybank a knock with his right leg. 'Let's go see a man about a drink,' he muttered encouragingly.

He hadn't changed much and some folk recognized him. He smiled with quiet amusement, as some stopped to stare, mutter suspicions or shake their heads. Most continued on about their business; one man called out something, whilst another ran for the saloon to spread the news that he was back.

Jesse was just as uncertain as they appeared to be, wondered what kind of greeting he'd get from his pa and Owen. He dismounted at the hitch rail outside of the saloon, glanced up at the name that was painted across a half-moon of sun-bleached timber. Wickett Saloon, it read. Below, it stated that Brent Marler was still the proprietor.

'See a man about a *free* drink,' Jesse

corrected himself. 'For ol' times sake.'

As though ready to leave quickly, men were already milling around the batwings. Someone indeed had spread the word of Jesse's arrival, and they drew back as he tied in the claybank and crossed the porch.

'Someone keep an eye on him. Hear tell there's a horse-thief in these parts,' he said, and winked in scheming humour as one man shrank away. In the saloon, a dozen or so drinkers at the bar fell silent, watched with cautious interest as he slapped dust from his jacket and pants. Jesse recognized one of them as Luke Bogan, a big man with long straw hair and a ruddy face. It was he who'd led the bunch of men who chased Jesse from town. Jesse mouthed a quiet curse as he reached the bar, considered a couple of fitting insults he could hurl, but nodded what he thought was easy recognition.

Brent Marler lumbered down the bar. He was balder now and he'd spread some. He sweated anxiously, mopped at his face with a cleaning towel.

'Howdy, gents,' Jesse said evenly. He leaned on the bar, glanced at Bogan then back at Marler. 'You goin' to stand an ol' friend a drink?'

Marler's eyes narrowed. 'Christ, Jesse, you got some neck,' he said. 'More'n two years since you quit town, an' the first thing you do is hit me for a free drink.' Most of the man's body wobbled as he chuckled outright. 'You come back to settle differences?' he added as he set up the round.

'The only differences we got, Brent, is that around *my* gut I'm carryin' a big Colt. You all look like it's the other way round.' With that, Jesse gave a tight, icy smile.

Marler nodded his acceptance of Jesse's joke. 'None of us are gunnies, Jesse. We're mostly friends in this town,' he replied.

'Good. I'll keep that in mind. Thank you,' Jesse said and turned to Luke Bogan. The man was sipping beer and his eyes were unmoving and steely as they looked at Jesse from above the rim of his glass 'So what're *you* doin', Luke? Ridin' with your own brand now?' he asked.

Bogan drained his glass before setting it down on the counter. Then he rolled the back of a cuff across his mouth. For a moment, Jesse thought he wasn't going to answer, but then the man leaned on the bar and turned his head slowly in Jesse's direction.

'I'm ramrod at the Triple T . . . ridin' for your old man,' he responded.

Jesse's jaw twitched and he ignored the drinks that Marler was setting before him. He was surprised, but kept his gaze firmly on Bogan. 'What happened to my brother Owen? He was foreman when I left.'

Bogan's expression didn't change. 'Havin' been away an' all, you won't have heard. Festus died. I guess it weren't long after you rode out.'

'Hell, Luke, that's his pa you're talkin' about,' Marler growled.

'What happened?' Jesse asked, as a knot suddenly formed in his stomach.

'Horse threw him off Buzzard Point,' Bogan responded evenly. 'He was up there chasin' strays.'

Jesse's eyes narrowed. 'It's a poor trail up there, but he was one o' the best horsemen in these parts.'

Bogan shrugged. 'Yeah, I know. But that don't amount to a hill o' beans when you disturb a big goddamn sidewinder. That's what sign showed.'

Jesse picked up his whiskey, and his hand trembled as he lifted the shot glass to his mouth. He tossed down the fiery liquid then took a sip of the beer chaser.

'No one knew where to find you, Jesse,' Marler said when Jesse looked at him. 'You never stayed in one place long enough to get word.'

Jesse took a thoughtful moment while he set down the beer. 'So my pa's dead, an' Owen's no longer foreman.'

Bogan nodded abruptly. 'Why'd you come back?' he asked, in a manner that suggested him and Jesse had never been friends.

'I got to wonderin' on changes . . rememberin' old friends,' Jesse replied, almost absently.

Bogan gave an uncaring smile. 'Shouldn't be too long a stay then,' he said and smiled again.

'Yeah,' Jesse agreed. 'You certainly make it all a bit less.'

'Another beer, Jesse?' Marler asked, auguring the temper of a fight.

'Thanks, but I've just about had enough o' this one. Either *that*, or the company. I'll ride out to the ranch . . . get me some fresh air.'

'You'll find no welcome mat,' Bogan growled.

'Maybe not. But it's still called the Triple T,' Jesse replied, and gave Bogan a long, withering look.

5

'Why not tell us the *real* reason you've come back to Wickett,' Luke Bogan scowled.

'I just told you,' Jesse replied. 'To see the civic improvements. That includes friends.'

Bogan's mouth twisted more. 'Goin' to take a look at the brat while you're here?'

Jesse froze, then took a deep breath. 'I've been gone two years, Bogan, so there will be some things I don't know about,' he started. 'It sounds like you're tryin' to tell me about one of 'em.'

Bogan made a casual gesture. 'The kid that good lookin' chilli bore you. Could be another reason you left town in such a hurry.'

Marler heard the sneer in Bogan's words, knew the man was itching for trouble. But he also saw the shock on Jesse's face.

'Right or wrong, Jesse, there were a few folk thought you must've known,' he offered in a conciliatory tone.

'I ain't too certain what's bein' said here,' Jesse replied, as he pushed off the bar to face Bogan. 'But if it's what I think, you best find some other way o' sayin' it.'

The big ramrod didn't look too worried as he faced him. 'You want to take somethin' out on me 'cause the world an' his dog knows you've sired a mixed blood?' he suggested with a crude laugh.

Very quickly Jesse's arm moved and his fist slammed into Bogan's mouth. The man knocked two cowboys aside as he staggered back along the bar. His lips had mashed back against his teeth and his mouth turned red as he clawed at the end of the bar for support. Then he hung there, blinking and gasping, as blood dripped from his chin.

'Ah hell, Jesse,' Marler said. The resignation was clear in his voice, that even with Bogan begging for trouble,

Jesse hadn't mellowed in the time he'd been away.

The saloon's early customers were already pressing in. They didn't care if Jesse had changed or not. They wanted to see a fight and they didn't much care what it was about or who it was between.

Bogan straightened slowly and put his hand to his mouth. He looked at the blood smeared across the back of it, then stared back along the bar at Jesse. 'I'll give you some other way,' he rasped and came charging back. He swept some glasses before him that Marler hadn't moved aside, grabbed the whiskey bottle and hurled it at Jesse.

Jesse was ready and stepped away from the bar, set himself for Bogan's rush. The two men thudded together, their bodies jarring with the short blows they delivered. They staggered back, grunting and gasping for breath, then went toe to toe, slugged away with short vicious punches. After a full minute, Jesse fell back against the bar. Bogan snatched a bottle from a table and leapt in, swung it wildly at Jesse's head.

Jesse rolled to one side and the bottle smashed and shattered on the glistening bartop. Whiskey was soaking his jacket as he swung a right hook to catch Bogan behind the ear. Off balance, the man's boots slipped in spilled drink and he stumbled. Jesse twisted his fingers in the man's long hair and twisted him around, slammed his forehead hard against the bar's panelling. Bogan's legs buckled and he went to his knees. Jesse booted him in the side of the head and the man fell to the floor, grunted and rolled on to his side.

Jesse took a breath, as if in challenge, looked at the men who stood around . . . and they took an instinctive step back.

Then Bogan kicked out and caught Jesse on the kneecap. With a raw sense of survival, Bogan rose up to butt Jesse in the face. As Jesse's leg collapsed, Bogan slugged away with his fists and elbows, driving in blows wherever he could. Jesse pushed himself away, tried to fend off Bogan, but his head was buzzing and he was disorientated. He rubbed his face, turned his back for a few seconds waiting for the haze to clear.

Bogan lashed out with his boots and caught Jesse high on the leg. The hurt was instant and excruciating, but, as it moved up into his body, it brought him painful reality. As Bogan threw himself at him again, he brought up both hands, clawed and grabbed at the enraged ramrod's shirt front. He swung his boot hard into the man's belly as he shoved him away, moved forward to take a measured swing. Bogan rolled backwards, coughed and spluttered in breathless agony as he crashed back against the solid front of the bar. He fell in a dazed heap, hooked one arm over the brass foot rail and dropped his head.

Jesse staggered to his feet as Bogan fought to stand. He pressed the heel of his boot against the ramrod's chest and held him down. Then with his left hand he hauled the man up, holding him steady, slammed his right fist into the flat of his face. He held on and, as Bogan's shirt ripped away, he punched twice again into the rough meat of his face. The man's nose flattened pulpily and a gash opened over one of his eyebrows. Bogan arched back across the bar and Jesse gritted his teeth, drove a fist hard into the offered stomach.

Bogan grunted, gurgled weakly through his nose before sliding along the bar. Then as his legs finally gave way, he collapsed, crumpled down to the dirty floor. With blood-glazed eyes, he glared briefly up at Jesse. Then in the sudden silence, he reached out both arms and spread himself into the dank sawdust.

Jesse swayed against the bar, gripped its edge firmly as Marler pushed a brimming glass of whiskey towards him.

'For medicinal purposes,' the saloon's proprietor said. 'Ain't nothin' more'n the doc would prescribe.'

Jesse lifted it with both hands and swallowed gratefully, winced as the spirit stung his split lips. 'That's what happens when you don't brawl regular. It kind o' gets saved up,' he replied.

'Well that explains it all then,' a voice behind him said coldly. 'I heard tell you hadn't changed.'

Jesse raised his eyes to the back bar mirror, met the bleak gaze of Sheriff John Turgoose.

6

Turgoose was a man in his late forties, soured by years of eking out a life around the limits of the Edwards Plateau. His face was deeply lined and his mouth was hidden beneath a thick, tobacco-stained moustache. The brass star that was pinned to his vest was the only thing about the man that was shiny clean, that and the butt of a big Dragoon Colt.

Jesse turned slowly, cursed quietly as he faced the man. 'Takin' an early turn, Sheriff?' he suggested wearily.

'Preservin' the peace,' Turgoose answered. 'That means findin' out what the hell you're doin' in town.'

'I was havin' a drink courtesy o' the establishment here, when Bogan disturbed my peace. Ask anyone.'

Turgoose flicked hard eyes towards Brent Marler. 'That right?' he asked.

'Yeah, in a manner o' speakin'.'

43

'I didn't ask about manners o' speakin'. I asked if it was right.'

Marler shrugged, look a little flustered. 'Well, yeah. Jesse *was* mindin' his business. Luke bad mouthed Lupin Contento, an' . . . well there's just so much, I guess . . . '

Turgoose turned to Jesse. 'Bogan put it to you there's a kid, did he? Is that it, Jesse? He put it to you sort o' clumsy?'

Jesse held himself steady 'Yeah. He needed teachin' manners,' he replied calmly. 'I was around.'

The sheriff studied Jesse for a short moment, nodded with implied understanding. 'Ain't no secret o' the upshot o' your affections, Jesse. An' there was some folk — me included — who wondered why you stayed away so long. You come back to see him, Jesse? Is that what you're doin' in town?'

'That'll do,' Jesse said for the want of anything more to offer.

Turgoose shifted his attention to Bogan. The man had started to move, slowly and painfully was being helped upright by two ranch hands.

The sheriff turned back to Jesse. 'I'll settle for that, 'cause it's your own personal business, Jesse,' he accepted. 'All the same, you got till the sun goes down.'

'For what?'

'To attend to that business. It's time enough to see your kid . . . whoever you want to see. But I don't want you around at full dark. Be gone, Jesse.'

'Now you listen, Sheriff, I ain't — ' Jesse started.

Turgoose grunted abruptly, took a short, menacing step forward. 'No, you listen to me, Jesse Tripp. I had a gutful o' you before. If it hadn't been for your pa steppin' in, you'd likely still be restin' up in the town jail. But with your pa dead an' your own brother not givin' a hang for your wellbein', I won't have the weight o' Triple T pressin' me any more. So, you go see whoever you want, but get done by sundown.'

'An' if I don't, Sheriff?' Jesse asked.

Turgoose half smiled, shook his head

45

in exasperation. 'I know if I dig deep enough in my desk drawer, I'll come up with at least one Wanted dodger on you, Jesse. You want to run the risk?'

The sheriff turned as Bogan sagged heavily against the bar, watched as Marler poured him a whiskey.

'Whatever argument you had with Jesse, it's finished, Luke,' he explained. 'I've advised him to be gone by sundown. I'm advisin' *you* to get back to the Triple T, right now.'

Bogan nodded to Marler as he took the whiskey, then stiffened at Turgoose's warning. He slammed the glass back down on the counter, and turned his battered face.

'I've just got me a drink. I'll go when I've done,' he challenged.

Turgoose nodded. 'That's when you swallow,' he said. 'Your day's over.' He faced the cowboys who were standing beside their foreman. 'You two see he gets back. He don't look too full o' beans.'

Bogan pushed himself clear of the

bar, but Turgoose quickly placed a hand against his chest. 'Best leave the drink,' he gritted.

Bogan muttered as he stepped unsteadily around the lawman. With his men close following, he threw a hostile glance in Jesse's direction, but Turgoose saw it was well spent.

When the three men had eased themselves out through the batwings, Turgoose nodded up at the wall clock behind the bar. 'An' your minutes are tickin' away,' he reminded Jesse.

'Wish I had a couple o' cow prodders to help me,' Jesse muttered. Then he bent a knee stiffly and picked up his hat. He punched it back into shape, jammed it back on his head and turned to Marler.

'Thanks for the medication. Next time I'll be payin',' he said.

In response, Marler brought his hand up from under the bar, nodded at the column of coins he clinked dully on the counter. 'You *could* pay me out o' this,' he suggested tentatively.

Jesse frowned. 'What's that?' he said.

'It's from the card game you played just before the trouble. There's no interest o' course, I ain't a goddamn bank. An' there was the cost o' Billy's burial . . . the marker,' Marler answered. 'It's your winnin's, Jesse, or near enough,' he continued, when he saw that Jesse still looked puzzled. 'Let's call it twenty dollars, even.'

Jesse stared at the money, then he took a silver dollar from the top and handed it back to Marler. 'Well, that'll pay for today's spillage. Thanks,' he said.

Marler shrugged. 'An' Lupin's got work at Gus Tawfey's place.'

'She left the Triple T?' Jesse asked with noticeable disappointment.

Marler looked down at the counter and spun the silver coin. 'Owen threw her off, or so they say. But I guess he wouldn't have wanted her there . . . you know . . . her expectin' like.'

Jess smiled crookedly. 'Yeah, that make sense. My brother was famous for his charity. What about Holly Cowan?

Is she still around?'

The expression on Marler's face suddenly changed and he looked up at the clock. Jesse realized that he'd touched on something that the saloon proprietor didn't want to talk about.

'It was she who married Owen,' Turgoose intervened. His big moustache moved, and Jesse guessed there was the hint of a tough smile underneath. 'You surely didn't expect her to wait around, did you? Not after you'd been mixin' it with the Contento girl.'

Jesse silently studied the lawman for a few long seconds, then he pocketed the coins and tugged the brim of his hat. 'Brent'll tell you, there's some things don't need explainin',' he said tersely.

Marler lifted a hand in acknowledgement, and Turgoose watched Jesse walk across to the batwings. 'Remember what I said, Jesse,' he called out. 'Till sundown.'

Jesse didn't pause or indicate he'd heard the sheriff's warning. He pushed

49

open the doors and went out into the fading light. Some of the men who'd watched the brawl stepped back as he untied the reins from the hitch rail. He thought someone called out a friendly sounding greeting, raised a hand to no one in particular and walked the claybank to the livery.

The hostler stared at him warily. 'Heard you was back . . . thought maybe it was someone joshin',' he said. 'So I guess you already tangled with Bogan?'

'The owner o' this mare's a short-tempered, mean son-of-a-bitch, who could likely turn up. So make sure you groom an' grain it,' was Jesse's answer.

'Which one o' you's goin' to pay, then?'

Jesse gave a tired smile and shook his head. He drew a coin from his pants pocket and flipped it hard towards the man's stomach.

The hostler threw out his hands and took a couple of steps backwards. 'I was only askin' . . . didn't mean anythin' by it,' he said, looking down at the reeking carpet of hay around his boots.

7

Tawfey's was a grub house where the usual clientele of itinerant, passer-through cowboys could eat and drink as much beef biscuit and belly wash coffee as they wanted for fifty cents. To the folk of Wickett, it was a well known fact that Gus Tawfey made his gain on the probability of no one ever wanting a second helping. The interior was predominantly scrubbed pine, but no amount of soap and bristle would ever eradicate the accumulation of stains from benches, tables and floor.

Jesse pushed open the screen door and went in, started at the reek of meat and cooking juices. The place was empty and Jesse gave a spare smile as he walked to the counter and thumbed the service bell.

With a revolting sniff, Gus Tawfey emerged from behind a smoke-grimed, fly curtain. He was very short and very fat, wore a greasy bandanna around the top of his head. He wrung pudgy hands into a grimy apron, raised his head and squinted at Jesse.

'Jeeesus, you look like Jesse Tripp,' he said, and touched his shirt pocket like he was looking for spectacles.

'Huh, featured him even more before I met up with Luke Bogan. How are you, Gus?' Jesse asked.

'Same as ever. Runnin' this place keeps me cured,' he replied, with a quick, wary glance behind him. 'When did you get back in town?'

'Less than an hour ago. Brent Marler told me I can find Lupin Contento here.'

Tawfey shuffled his feet, lifted the edge of his apron to wipe something off the counter top. 'Yeah, she keeps the place lookin' tidy ... does some cookin' now an' again.'

'What's she doin' at the moment?' Jesse asked.

'Busy gettin' ready for the supper trade. Maybe I could get you somethin' if you want to wait. We're doin' beef stuff.'

Jesse smiled. 'If I want to poison myself, Gus, I'll do it with jimson. At least it'll be memorable.'

'Hey!' Tawfey called, as Jesse moved around the corner of the counter. 'Where you goin?' He made to block Jesse's way, but quickly thought better of it.

Jesse pushed his way through the curtain into the messy back kitchen. He cursed quietly, stopped to look around. On the far side of the room, a slim, dark-haired girl was stirring one of two large pots. She brushed the back of her forearm across her sweating forehead as pungent steam rose to her face. Jesse recognized Lupin Contento, but he was shocked at what he saw. Lupin looked older than her twenty years, her face was tight and drawn. She had lost weight, and the simple one-piece dress hung loose and shapeless from her body.

'Hello, Lupin,' he said quietly. 'It's me, Jesse.'

Lupin jumped, looked up sharply

through the rising vapours. For a moment, a smile flashed and her dark eyes lit with genuine warmth. She rested the big wooden ladle across one of the pots, turned and stepped towards Jesse. But she stopped a few feet short of him, and the smile disappeared when she looked over his shoulder.

'Don't you go lettin' that meat settle,' Tawfey said, and the girl's shoulders dropped as she turned unhappily back to the pots.

'Your front window needs a cloth takin' to it,' Jesse told the man, sharply.

Tawfey was breathing heavily. He looked anxious, but stood his ground. 'This is my kitchen. I come an' go as I please,' he retaliated.

Jesse nodded, cursed again, and walked towards Lupin. He took her arm and eased her towards the yard door. 'Then we'll step out back,' he said.

'If she goes out there with you, she stays out,' Tawfey threatened. 'I'm still the boss here.'

Jesse paused with the door half open, returned a chilly stare. 'All I want to do is talk to her. If I hear you've fired her, I'll come back with a beaver knife an' put your pieces in them cook pots. You understand, Gus?'

A little of the blood drained from Tawfey's face. He swallowed hard, clenched his trembling hands. 'Steady there, Jesse,' he muttered feebly. 'It's just, there's some boys who like the kind o' meat she puts on a plate.'

Jesse led the girl into the littered alley of empty crates and garbage. She stood with her back against the wall, looked anxiously back towards the open yard door.

Jesse reached out a supportive hand, but she refused to look at him. 'Hey come on, forget Tawfey,' he said genially. 'He ain't goin' to fire you . . . or anythin'. He knows I'll see to that.'

'Yes, I'm sure you will, Jesse. So, what is it you want?' she said, but still refused to look at him.

He reached out and turned her face, looked directly into her eyes. 'I'm told the world an' his dog believes I'm the father o' your kid,' he began. 'Only trouble is, Lupin, you an' me know that could never be. So, I'm naturally wonderin' on the whys an' wherefores.'

Jesse felt a shudder pass through Lupin's body, then her face crumpled and her chin fell forward. He let her take in a sobbing breath then turned her face up to him again.

'His name's Manolito, and I never said you were the father, Jesse,' she said huskily. 'I didn't mean for it to happen. You ran out, and somehow it just got around that you were the father. You were running wild, Jesse. You had a reputation, and it was easy for folk to think it was true. I just didn't say it wasn't, and for that I'm sorry. I didn't think it would hurt you.'

'Didn't the *real* father have anythin' to say? Why didn't he come forward?'

Jesse felt that Lupin had taken a grip on his arm.

'Why should he?' she asked. 'Being a father would have ground-hitched him. Huh, I'd be trouble enough. I don't blame him for not saying anything.'

'That don't stop him from makin' support. Has he given you much . . . or the kid? You don't look like you're livin' too high off any hog.'

Lupin hesitated then shook her head. 'It hasn't been easy. No one wanted anything to do with me. I couldn't get work, except here.'

'Yeah, I heard somethin' like that,' Jesse said thoughtfully. 'Why the hell didn't you quit Wickett? There's other towns . . . I've seen some of 'em.'

'Have you seen one that'll welcome an unmarried girl with a babe in arms? Besides, you need money to get to those other towns.'

'Surely you haven't worked here for nothin'? That meat-head pays you, doesn't he?'

'Yes, he pays. But most of it goes on Mano. I'm paying a woman to look after him, while I work. I eat here sometimes . . . all I want for fifty cents.' Lupin smiled with a little humour. 'A cruel circle, eh Jesse?' she said.

Jesse nodded, returned an understanding smile. 'Yeah, I guess there ain't much left for a wardrobe. Hell, Lupin, if he's still around, why haven't you squared up to the father?' he asked, and felt something uneasy gnawing away inside him.

'Maybe I could have done, but it's too late now, with everyone believing you're the father . . . *me* letting them believe it. If I suddenly changed my mind with the truth, it would make big trouble for Mano's father. He's quite an important man now . . . married and respectable.'

'Huh. Important an' married, maybe. But I'd wonder on the respectable bit. Tell me his name,' Jesse quickly put in. 'In the circumstances, I reckon I've a right to know. You ain't runnin' up a flag, 'cause you ain't sure who the father really is, are you, Lupin?' he suggested.

8

Jesse snapped his head back as Lupin's hand caught him a stinging blow across the side of his face. He caught her wrists as she tried to have another go with her other hand.

'I'm sorry I said that,' he rasped. 'But you can't blame me for thinkin' it. Goddamnit, Lupin, I wasn't the only one with a reputation for fun. What's sauce for the goose, eh?'

Jesse drew Lupin close, smiled crookedly as she squirmed. 'I guess you just got too close to the fire, eh, Lupin? You got what you get for tuggin' a feller's rope.'

'I was never a tease, Jesse, you know that. Mano's father had feelings for me, I know he did.'

'Yeah, well whoever he is, I hope the son-of-a-bitch's yellow streak ain't inherited by the kid.' Once again, Jesse felt a tenuous, uneasy misgiving. 'Sad in a way,' he added. 'For an hour or so, I'd seen myself as a pappy.'

Lupin relaxed, raised herself to give Jesse a quick kiss on the cheek.

'Somethin' else I've collected for old times' sake,' he muttered wryly.

'Will you come to see Mano? Tonight, when I finish here?'

Jesse looked uncertain, hesitant. 'Turgoose wants me out o' town by sundown, an' he's just itchin' for me to overstay. I ain't rilin' him any more than need be . . . not just yet anyways.'

'I understand,' Lupin said, disappointedly. 'But you're going out to Triple T?'

'Yeah. That's family, Lupin. I heard what happened to Pa.'

'And Holly? You heard about her?'

Jesse nodded. 'An' I never got me an invite to the weddin'. Never figured my brother as the marryin' kind, either. Still, shows how wrong you can be about some folk.'

'Why don't you just ride on? Seems

60

there's nothing much to keep you.' Lupin suggested tentatively and without looking directly at him.

'I never did aim to come back here, Lupin. I kind o' got bulldogged. But now I am here, an' despite Sheriff Turgoose, I'll stay till I'm good an' ready.'

'But you just said he wanted you gone by sundown.'

'Yeah, an' I will be . . . to the ranch. But I don't think he said anythin' about not returnin' to town. I'll see what Owen has to say.'

'He's got a big ranch now, Jesse. Much bigger than when your father was alive.'

'Hmm. I'll wager he's bigger on respectability too, eh Lupin?' Jesse suggested as the qualm niggled again.

'I haven't worked out there for a long time.'

'Since he fired you, you mean?'

Lupin nodded. 'I understand how he felt. He couldn't very well have me working around the house looking like a

pot-gutted cow. And Miss Holly didn't — '
She broke off.

'Miss Holly didn't what? Jesse asked
brusquely.

'Didn't want me around either,'
Lupin said, and shrugged.

Jesse thought for a moment. 'No, I
guess not,' he agreed with a knowing
look. 'I didn't know about Pa dying
. . . never would have figured him
cashin' out like that. He must've
encountered plenty o' snakes in his life.'
Jesse didn't say any more about his
father's death when it looked like Lupin
had something to say. 'What you
thinkin'?' he asked.

Lupin shook her head swiftly. 'Noth-
ing. I guess it was his luck running out.
Your father was a rough man, Jesse, but
I know there was another side to him.'

Jesse grinned crookedly. 'Tripps are
from the same pool all right, but that
don't mean we're all the same. We don't
all get into the same scrapes.'

'Or out of,' Lupin quipped back quietly.
Then Gus Tawfey's back door opened,

and the man stood there, impatient and irritable. 'Hey there, I said I needed help in the kitchen,' he started. 'You goin' to keep her talkin' all day, Jesse? *You* might not have responsibilities . . . I do.'

'If you mean what it sounds like you mean, you best keep worryin' about what I said earlier,' Jesse rasped back. 'An' now, when Lupin steps back into your goddamn grease joint, you're payin' her a couple o' dollars a week *more*. You got that?'

Tawfey sniffed, cursed under his breath and nodded tetchily.

'Smart,' Jesse said and turned to Lupin. 'I'll look in on young Mano, soon as I get a chance,' he added, but louder for Tawfey's benefit, 'an' I like the name,' and winked.

Guessing the real reason for what Jesse had just said, Lupin smiled back. From what Gus Tawfey had just seen and heard, the man would waste no time in confirming what every other person in town had always suspected . . . that Jesse

Tripp was indeed the father.

'Thanks,' she mouthed, and returned to stir the pots of meat, add some potatoes and onions.

*   *   *

Shadows were lengthening as Jesse stepped out of the alley into the main street. He saw John Turgoose standing on the veranda of the law office. The sheriff took out his stem winder and held it out towards him. Then he tapped the face of it, gestured to where the sun was dipping towards the Sierra Blancas.

Jesse waved back casually, and walked on to the livery where he collected the claybank. The hostler stayed well out of the way as he saddled up and rode out. He sat the mount a spell and looked along the deeply coloured, shadowy street, wondered the whereabouts of the shirt-tail rancher who'd been chasing him. He guessed the man must have turned tail and returned home. He went on to Wickett's Mercantile and smiled as he saw Turgoose hurrying towards him, wittingly ignored the lawman's call as he entered the general store.

He was already paying for a sack of tobacco and papers when the sheriff pushed irately through the store's glass-panelled door. The storekeeper, an incongruously dapper, suited man, held up both hands and waved them in the air.

'All damages get paid for, lawful business or not,' he stated bravely.

Jesse almost looked amused as he snapped a coin on to the counter. 'Evenin', Sheriff. I'm just buyin' me some Bull Durham. Quality picks up when you got money,' he said, turning to face Turgoose.

'Must make a change from shredded horse turds,' Turgoose replied. 'But in case you hadn't noticed, it's almost sundown.'

'Yeah, I had noticed,' Jesse answered evenly. 'Still time enough for provisions.'

'There's somethin' else I can get you?' the storekeeper asked uneasily.

Jesse nodded. 'I need coffee an' bacon. An' some tinned milk an' some peaches, if you got 'em.' Then he grinned at Turgoose. 'Havin' money in my pocket don't happen too often.'

'I'm just glad you're hittin' the trail,' Turgoose said drily.

'How much do I owe you?' he asked the storekeeper.

'Two dollars an' five cents. Call it two even . . . for cash.'

Jesse went outside and built a cigarette, sat on the top of the steps and smoked it down, slowly. Sheriff Turgoose leaned on the rail at the other end of the veranda, impatiently tapped his fingers.

Ten minutes later, Jesse was tying his sack of provisions behind the saddle when Turgoose stepped forward.

'Christ, you're pushin' your luck, Jesse Tripp,' he gritted.

'Just thankful for every minute, Sheriff,' Jesse answered back. He mounted, nodded at the storekeeper who was standing in his doorway, and one or two inquisitive townsfolk, then he walked the horse easily down the street. As he cleared the edge of town, the sun finally disappeared and he gave a shiver. John Turgoose cursed, then made his way back to his office.

9

Supper was way past, when Jesse arrived at the Triple T. The bunkhouse was in darkness, but lamps burned in the cookshack where the cook was preparing food for the morning, and other lights blazed bright yellow in the big house.

The building was just as he remembered it, except for one end. His father had built a low rambling adobe annexe, but now there was an upper floor at the southern end. There were still two barns and three corrals, the water tanks, animal pens, chicken coops and the bunkhouse — or 'dice-house' as his father referred to it.

He sat at the hogback rise a little longer, recalled some of the times he'd spent with his father and brother, then he nudged the claybank down towards the house. As he started to dismount in

68

the home yard, a man with a carbine stepped out of the shadows.

'Just hold up there, Jesse,' Luke Bogan said, through his split lips. 'You ain't been invited, an' this ain't no welcome party. I told you as much in town.'

Jesse paused, and then swung his leg over the saddle and stepped down. He heard Bogan work the lever of his carbine, but draped the mount's reins over the rails and turned slowly.

'Go tell my brother I'm here,' he said. 'I take it you're his messenger.'

'He don't want to see you,' Bogan snapped back. 'You're trouble an' everybody knows it. He said I was to send you on your way, if you showed.'

Jesse smiled. 'I can think o' reasons why he'd have wanted that, but he certainly wouldn't have asked you to take care of it. Not if he knew about our little meetin' in town, earlier.'

With that, Jesse stepped on to the porch. As Bogan backed up, he turned swiftly, grabbed the short barrel of the carbine and snatched it violently from his hands.

'Last time it was fists, Bogan. If you want to make it guns, that's fine with me,' he challenged. He brought the short barrel up, pressed it hard under Bogan's rough chin. 'But it would be real stupid.'

Then the door of the house opened and Jesse immediately recognized the silhouette of his brother. In the lighted hall, he also saw Holly, standing behind him.

'Hello, Owen,' he said calmly. With the carbine in his right hand, he gestured behind to Bogan. 'Your ramrod just got through tellin' me you didn't want to see me. Well, that's right unneighbourly, Brother, seein' as how long it's been.'

'Just invite him in, Owen,' Holly said flatly. 'Luke, you go see to the night rounds.'

'Obliged, an' thank you kindly, Mrs Tripp,' Jesse said, and nodded as he stepped into the house. 'There's a heap o' stuff to talk about . . . a whole heap o' stuff.' He glanced quickly at Holly as he walked into the lighted hall, through the door of the front parlour.

Jesse looked around him, felt a curious, rising wave of nostalgia. 'Let's talk . . . you can tell me what happened to Pa,' he said when Owen and Holly entered the room.

'I will, when you put that goddamn carbine, down. You forgettin' where you are?' Owen snapped.

'Yeah, for a moment,' Jesse replied. Then he grinned, laid the gun across a near side table. 'There's a little brand stamp on the stock, if I recall. I'd say it belongs in *my* war sack more than it does in Bogan's.'

Owen was as tall as his brother and carried a strong facial resemblance. He scowled as he moved to the drinks. 'Then you can have it,' he said. 'There's a saddle scabbard somewhere in the barn. Look it out when you leave.' Owen's hand was shaking, and the bourbon decanter clinked several times against the rim of the glasses as he poured three drinks.

Jesse and Holly took their glasses, Holly lifted hers in a brief salute. 'I suppose someone should say 'welcome home', Jesse,' she said quietly.

Jesse's voice was cool in response. 'Why do I get the feelin' that that ain't a shared sentiment?' he said.

Owen tossed down the rich liquor and poured another. 'Holly's speakin' for herself. I ain't been holdin' my breath waitin' for you to show.'

Jesse laughed. 'Family feelin', eh? Must admit, I was never goin' to bust a gut to get back, either.'

'Then why did you?'

'Circumstances, Owen. I was in Wickett an' heard a few things that needed more of an explanation. Pa's death was one of 'em.'

The younger Tripp dropped wearily into a button-back to drink his Kentucky bourbon, but Holly remained standing. She was a tall girl, her grey-blue eyes almost on a level with

Jesse's. Her long fair hair hung in curls and her dress cost more than a cowpoke earned in three months, probably what Lupin Contento made in six. Jesse could see that Triple T was prospering a deal more so than when Festus Tripp was alive.

'It was an accident . . . pure bad luck,' Owen said. 'Rattler takin' the sun on the cliff trail above the canyon. Horse shied an' Pa must've been caught off his guard. Likely he was watchin' steers down in the canyon . . . maybe makin' a count. There was some blood, where we figured he must have hit his head. Hopefully he was unconscious when he went over the edge.' Owen paused to take another big sip of his drink. He bared his teeth, looked mournfully at the cow hide rug under his feet. 'We didn't find him till nearly first dark. That long in the sun . . . it weren't a pretty picture.'

Jesse grunted his understanding. 'No one went up Buzzard Point with him? He went alone?' he asked.

Owen nodded, continued his downward stare. 'We set out from here, together. Fact is, he decided he wanted me to go flush some slicks from the foothills. So I did . . . there weren't no need for an argument.' The man banged a fist down on the arm of the chair. 'But I should have been with him.'

'Even if he was makin' a tally, it was odd for any o' Pa's mounts to be caught off guard. Still, from what you say happened, I guess no one could've saved him.'

Holly glanced sharply at her husband, then flicked her bright eyes to Jesse's sober face.

Owen lifted an arm as if to emphasize something, but let it fall. 'Yeah, I know it, but maybe there was somethin' I could have done. I didn't even give him a thought, until he didn't show here.' Owen slowly looked up at Jesse. There was a new tension that pinched his features, and he faltered when he continued, 'The ranch . . . it was left to me,' he said, then quickened, sounding as though he didn't want to give his brother the chance to query what he was saying. 'I mean, you an' Pa never did get along. He was left mighty riled at the way you quit town after Billy Hugh was shot. You never said goodbye . . . not to him, me or anyone.'

Jesse's eyes grew more wary. 'You both knew I was capable o' that. It shouldn't have surprised you too much,' he said levelly. 'An' I wouldn't say we never got along. Sure he tore the odd strip off me, gave me a good larrupin', now an' again, but that weren't much more'n larkin'. Pa an' me weren't the kind who'd say how we felt for each other. Not like you an' me, eh, Owen?'

When Holly glanced again at her unsettled, fidgety husband, Jesse had the distinct feeling that there was something going unsaid.

Owen disregarded Jesse's dig about family feelings. 'Morgan Samwell's got a copy of the will, if you want to see it,' he said. 'Pa left you five hundred dollars, cash. Samwell's been holdin' it 'cause we've never known where to send it.'

'Yeah, someone in town said somethin' similar,' Jesse replied a little edgily. 'I guess the money was Pa's little conscience absolvin' gift. But there was no need, an' I ain't upset or offended that he left the spread to you, Owen.'

'I knew you wouldn't be,' Holly said, and made a slight smile. 'After all, Owen had the permanence . . . the sense of responsibility. It was him who stayed around an' helped run the place while you were off to Lord knows where . . . gettin' up to Lord knows what. It was only fittin'.'

'You don't need to explain, Holly,' Jesse retorted, 'considerin' it ain't really any o' your business.'

In reality, Jesse was a bit disappointed that his father hadn't left him something more substantial — something to show that he had cared. Still the money had value, and there was

76

something he could use it for. He'd never come by so much money in one day in his whole life, he wanted to tell them, thought it best to keep quiet. He was also disappointed, a bit irked at the support that Holly was giving his brother.

'Why *did* you come back, Jesse?' Holly asked abruptly.

'Seems that's what a lot o' folk in these parts want to know,' he replied.

'They probably think you're on the run. Are you Jesse? Have you rode out here to pick up the owl-hoot?'

'East, west, home's best. Didn't our ma used to say that?' Jesse responded. 'Huh, makes you wonder, don't it? Pa an' the ranch gone, even Lupin's made herself another life.' Jesse watched for another shared look between Owen and Holly. He caught a fleeting movement, wondered how much they wanted him gone.

'Sorry, did you say somethin'?' he asked Holly, thinking maybe she had.

'I was goin' to ask if you wanted to

stay for the night. Our housemaid can make up a room . . . your old one if you want.'

Jesse's first instinct was to tell them both to go to hell. But he figured Holly was counting on that, and he didn't want to give her the satisfaction. He'd already let her rattle him with her assurance and comfort in his old home.

'Yeah, thanks. My old room will be just fine. In fact, I might stick around for a couple o' days. Take a look around . . . see if there's any fish to catch up in the pools. I could even ride on to Buzzard Point,' he said in an attempt to provoke his younger brother.

'Why the hell would you want to go up there? That place ain't exactly full o' happy memories,' Owen responded as Jesse thought he might.

Jesse smiled back artfully. 'You don't know where any o' my memories lie, Brother, happy or otherwise,' he said.

'Luke Bogan won't like you hangin' around.'

Jesse shook his head. 'Now that's

somethin' that *really* don't concern me, Owen. But if you want to keep your foreman usefully employed, I happen to know they got one or two pedigree bulls for sale in Chimney Point.'

'Well, your advice really ain't needed here any more, Jesse,' Holly intervened. 'Whether it's on Luke Bogan or breed cattle.'

'I'll go an' see the grave,' Jesse decided. 'If Bogan tries to stop me doin' *that*, he'll die. I don't mean to bring any trouble, but that's an iron-bound promise,' he warned icily. Then he picked up the carbine. 'If you want to keep the peace, you figure somethin' out. It's your ranch,' he offered. 'I'll be outside. I saw there was still primroses beyond the home pasture. Scent drifts in kindly on a night breeze, I recall.'

'Don't go causin' us any trouble, Jesse. *You* might not have changed, but we all have,' Holly huffed, as he moved to the door. 'Owen would be quite within his rights to have you removed from the ranch.'

'You can remove one o' them Ts from the title,' Jesse scowled caustically as he watched his brother pour another drink.

As Jesse closed the door, he heard Holly's few stern words. 'An' that's enough for tonight,' she said.

'Go eat worms,' Owen growled back, and Jesse heard the muted clink of glass.

He turned the claybank into the nearest corral and sat on the stoop, smoked quietly until the housemaid told him his room was ready.

★ ★ ★

Much later, when the rest of the house was quiet and in darkness, Jesse closed the door to the room where he'd grown up. He lit a table lamp and looked around at what now seemed to be a storeroom. The broken skull of a bighorn was missing, as was his Yellowboy hunting rifle and the fishing pole his father had given him for one of his early birthdays. But a coloured print he'd pinned on the wall was still there, and an illustration of two men riding in amongst buffalo, shooting at close range with long-barrelled Colts. And torn from the front pages of dime novels, there was a portrait of a notorious gunfighter, pictures of Indians riding wild-eyed mustangs, bareback. He gave a wry smile. In later, more recent years, he'd turned some of those imaginary tales into fact, especially gunfighting and brawling.

The room smelled musty, unused, and his old pine highboy was now stuffed with tally books and other ranch papers. In one drawer, he found a tintype image of his mother and father. The boys standing beside his mother were him and Owen. He looked at the fading brown figures and saw the strong resemblance between himself and his father, although Festus Tripp had sported a heavy drooping moustache. There was a resemblance to Owen, as well, but the younger brother bore a softer look, his mother's eyes.

He gently prised the thin sheet of metal from its frame and put it in his inside jacket pocket. The small picture looked like being the only significant connection with his past life that he was going to get hold of, and he'd be riding off with *that*.

Jesse lifted the window to let in some cool air, but he was a long time falling asleep. The last time he'd slept in the room was the night before he'd gone to town with Billy Hugh. Now, the memories crowded in on him again.

Trouble was, the townfolk of Wickett were so accepting of Jesse Tripp getting into trouble, that not one of them actually considered which one of the two erstwhile friends had actually kicked off the fight — the fight that ended with Billy coughing out his life in the hard-packed dirt of the main street.

10

It was the ranch waddies saddling up in the yard that stirred Jesse. A little rested but no less tired, he drew up the window blind, saw it was just after first light. Issuing the day's chores, Luke Bogan was waving his hat in all directions, snapping orders to the hands.

Jesse sat beside the window and built a cigarette. He smoked it thoughtfully and leisurely, listened to the sounds of the men riding from the yard. When he heard the noise of pots and pans rattling from the house kitchen, he pulled on his boots and went out to wash at the bench by the back door.

'Fittin' for a saddle-tramp . . . a goddamn itinerant,' he spluttered cynically then went into the kitchen. Two Mexican house helps he'd never seen before were preparing breakfast for

Holly and Owen. He joked with them in rough Spanish, sat at a table out of the way and sipped the coffee they poured him. Neither of them had been here when his father had died, but one remembered the day Lupin was fired, and it took a considerable amount of Jesse's charm to get her to talk about it.

'The boss told her to go,' she started nervously. 'He was throwing things around, and shouting. He was very angry you know.'

'Yeah, I can imagine as how,' Jesse said encouragingly. 'Do you know if she had any money?' Jesse asked. 'She must have been owed some.'

'Well, he shouted for her to buy a stagecoach ticket out of town . . . said that twenty dollars would get her to El Paso or Sweetwater, Texas.'

'What else did the boss shout?'

'He warned her not to ever come near the ranch again.'

Jesse cursed softly. 'Was Holly around?' he asked.

The girl shook her head, looked

anxiously towards the door. 'No, not then. But I think the boss marrying her, was what got him calmed down.'

'How'd you mean?'

'When he found out Lupin stayed in town and didn't buy a coach ticket, my, such anger, and for such a time.'

Jesse smiled and thanked them for talking to him. Then, deep in thought, he ate a breakfast platter of eggs and fried corn.

Straight after eating, he went to get the scabbard for the carbine, then down to the corral to saddle the claybank. He was surprised that Holly was already there, and wearing an outfit for riding.

'Good mornin', Jesse. Where are you intendin' to ride?' she asked in a pleasant enough manner.

'I thought I'd see just how much the ol' place has spread out,' he said.

'Curiosity then? I mean, you no longer have any interest, financial or otherwise.'

Again, Jesse sensed he was being provoked, and he puffed in irritation.

'The otherwise bit, ain't true, Holly. An' never could be. Can I saddle you a horse, for wherever it is you're goin'?'

'The bay mare, thank you. I'm waitin' on a Tennessee Walker. Owen's gettin' it shipped here from Kentucky.'

Jesse shook out a rope and looked at her coolly. 'Yep, the place must be doin' all right. Pure bloodstock, eh?' he muttered in appreciation.

'Very all right,' Holly responded with a superior smile. 'If you want, I'll ride with you. I imagine you'll be goin' to your father's grave. He's next to your mother, naturally.'

A half-hour later, they reached the low, grass-covered knoll where Tripps were buried. Jesse didn't dismount, but Holly did. She went to the graveside and turned a confused face towards him. Jesse quietly sat the claybank, looked down at the gravestone that bore his father's name. Then he looked at the more weathered stone with his mother's name and a much smaller grave of a sister he could barely remember.

'They look well tended,' he said quietly, as if to no one in particular.

'I make sure one of the hands comes out here, regular,' she replied.

'That's good, Holly,' he responded with obvious sincerity. 'It's gettin' to be quite a family plot. If somethin' happens to me — an' it's possible — I'd like to be brought back here, supposin' there's enough left o' me.'

'Many a true word, eh Jesse?' she said, mounting up again. 'But who'd want to pay for it?'

He said nothing more, kicked his heels to catch up with her. For another fifteen minutes she led them across a series of hills, then reined in on boulder strewn rising ground. When Jesse walked the claybank alongside her bay, she pointed down to where Cotton-wood Creek bent in its course.

'That's Triple T land, as far as you can see,' she claimed proudly.

Jesse whistled with surprise. 'What happened to the spreads along the river bottoms? There were four or five. The

Jukes an' McLanes an' Donovans were there.'

'We bought 'em. Them, an' some others to the west. An' there's Billy Hugh's old place.'

'Hell, that must've taken a barnload o' money. An' then some.'

'No, I don't believe it did,' she said, and looked away a little flustered. 'Owen was able to get good prices on all the property.'

'I didn't grow up yesterday, Holly,' Jesse countered. 'That's another way o' sayin' somethin' weren't exactly four square.'

'I don't know about that . . . didn't ask for details,' she answered offhandedly. 'Owen's a good businessman, *that* I do know. He's almost doubled the size o' the ranch. Whichever way he's achieved it, it's done, an' it's made him an influential citizen. He's not to be dickered with any more, Jesse. You'd best remember that.'

'I remember he's my brother before all else,' Jesse said. Then he leaned

88

across and gripped Holly's wrist. 'What's with all these slights an' threats, Holly? What is it that's got you so proddy? Do you figure I've come back to fight over the will? Is that it?'

Holly nodded uncertainly. 'It's Owen. He feels guilty. He's been expectin' you to show up, an' here you are,' she said quietly, but now there was the mien of relief in her look.

'If Pa thought I was worth five hundred dollars, well that's what I'm worth. I ain't goin' to fight Owen or anybody over it,' Jesse explained. 'Believe me, I've got enough trouble. I really ain't after more.'

'Do you want to ride down to the river? We're close to where we used to visit,' Holly said by way of response.

Jesse was halfway through saying yes, but suddenly changed his mind. 'Er, I guess not,' he replied.

The put-out look was back on Holly's face again. 'Doesn't the high grass along the bank remind you of anythin'? That hidey-hole under the cutbank, where you're hidden from the world?'

'Yeah, it reminds me, Holly. But now you're married to my brother, for Chris' sake. An' I just told you, I don't want any more trouble.'

Holly's face continued with its intriguing changes of expression. 'An' if I wasn't married to Owen? What then?' she wanted to know.

'Well you *are*, an' that's that,' Jesse responded with a shake of his head.

'It's to do with Lupin Contento an' her *niño*,' she carped. 'Your *niño*, Jesse. Good God, as if I hadn't suffered enough humiliation on *her* behalf, I'm bringing it on myself, now.'

'At least there's no one except me to see it this time, Holly, an' I'll pretend it never happened. An' as for sufferin', it's only Lupin that's doin' that, from what I've seen.'

With that, Jesse wheeled to turn the claybank away from the rising ground. 'An' I aim to do somethin' about that,' he muttered portentously.

'Tell Owen, I'll see him sometime.'

After a few moments, Holly let out a long breath. 'I hope you ain't goin' to do anythin' stupid,' she said to herself.

Jesse was angry because, like the others, Holly was so ready to believe he was the father of Lupin's child. Hell, he thought, she wasn't much more than a button, herself.

On a town heading, he spurred into the stands of ash and juniper. Finding that Holly and his brother had married, let alone to each other, had shaken him. And it had all happened within a few months of him leaving. But Jesse brightened then, and smiled. Yeah, she's been pinin', he told himself. She still was. She'd just taken the edge of it by marrying Owen.

Jesse reined in the claybank. He sat in the peace and quiet of the timber, and his thoughts went on to Billy Hugh. It was Holly mentioning the Hugh place, that did it. For the umpteenth time, he recalled the last moments he'd shared with Billy on that fateful night.

They'd both of them been drunk, but it was Billy who'd started the trouble. He was ornery because Jesse had beaten him fair and square at blackjack, and he didn't want Jesse to celebrate — not with the girl, anyway. So Billy had got mad. He wouldn't give in, kept pushing Jesse until he was forced to stop him. 'For Chris' sake, Billy, she was a goddamn chippy,' Jesse said aloud. 'She weren't interested in you. It was my goddamn winnin's she was after.'

He cursed loudly, kicked the clay-bank's flanks, got it moving out of the trees and *en route* for Wickett.

After he'd shot Billy, a bunch of cowpokes had pursued him to the timberline of the Blancas. He knew that he shouldn't have continued to run, that he should have gone back to straighten things out, but instead, he'd continued to ride north. The thought of returning home became more and more distant as time wore on.

Yeah, now that everything was lost or spoken for, it looked like he'd been a fool to get anywhere near the road back. So, he'd do some business in Wickett, get John Turgoose stirred up a tad, and then he'd ride. He drew the tintype from his pocket, looked at it for a short while before climbing back on the claybank.

A minute later the rifle cracked a shot out from the trees and the horse snorted with shock, crowhopped several feet away from the trail. Jesse hauled up instinctively, cursed while reaching behind him for the carbine. The rifle in the trees behind him fired again, and this time he felt the thump and burn of the bullet as it creased his neck.

'Christ, I'd forgotten you,' he rasped out.

He felt the sticky blood on his neck as he freed the carbine and went sideways, down from the saddle. He hit the ground hard, threw himself behind a big, blowdown tree root, and gasped at the pain of landing. He cursed again, squirmed lower as another bullet kicked up a divot.

He levered a round up into the carbine's chamber and looked for gunsmoke. But in the light breeze, the smoke had drifted thin among the timber and he had no sign of the ambusher's position. Then he saw it when the gun opened up again. There was a rapid, four shot volley, and bark shards and dirt stung his wounded neck. 'No, you ain't the goddamn hoe man,' he muttered.

He felt something move against his leg, looked down and gasped loudly. Then he shuddered with revulsion as a hognose slithered quickly towards his foot. He lashed out, kicked wildly as the snake turned away into the shelter of the old gnarled roots. 'Leave us alone. What is it with you lot an' Tripps?' he seethed.

He took a few, quick shallow breaths, figured the man was now reloading. Thinking it was his chance, he pushed himself into a crouching position and brought up the carbine. But the dogged rifleman had been waiting for such a move and he triggered off another shot. Jesse spun backwards as the lead tore through the loose underarm folds of his jacket. His carbine exploded skywards and he dived back down behind the stump for cover. With his ears ringing and his heart thumping, he closed his eyes for a moment. 'So who the hell are you?' he wondered.

He heard a horse running away through the timber and he rolled from his cover once again. Coming up on one knee with the carbine's stock already pressed tight to his shoulder, he sighted quickly. He saw the rider as he moved away through the shadowy trees, and he resolutely squeezed off two shots, then another, while the echoes resounded dully. The bullets smashed and cracked through the branches, leaves flew, and for a moment he focused on a broken branch and listened. But he couldn't see much, only sensed that the rider had fled, was deeper into the thick timber.

'If it's you, Owen, I never touched

her,' he shouted. Then he pulled his hat back on and ran for the claybank. 'Bet this ain't the sort o' work you're used to,' he rasped, looking the animal in its dark, anxious eyes. He pushed the carbine back into its scabbard, vaulted into the saddle and dug his heels.

By the time Jesse had reached a break in the timber, there was no sight or sign of the ambusher. But with such proficient shooting, Jesse was certain he'd escaped a would-be killer. Sitting thoughtfully, he couldn't even hear the man's horse now. He cursed, turned his neck scarf carefully against his bleeding neck.

'If there's someone tryin' to kill me, least I can do is play the game. Turgoose can go kick his own dog. I ain't broke any laws yet, so why *should* I ride on?'

11

Jesse stopped on the sidewalk and took a careful look around him. From up and down the street, he speculated on the chances of someone having him in their gun sights. 'No, not likely, we're back in civilization,' he mumbled wryly. But he was entering the building where Morgan Samwell had his office, when John Turgoose called out his name.

He expected the run in, but he'd made up his mind not to be intimidated by Turgoose or anyone else until he knew what was going on. There were quite a few questions needing answers, and he wasn't going to leave Wickett until he had them. Jesse set himself for trouble and turned to face the sheriff.

Turgoose was staring straight at him as he made to direct some folk aside. 'What the hell are you doin' back in town?' the man growled. 'I thought I told you to ride on.'

Jesse looked unperturbed as he shaped up. 'You'll strain somethin' you go on like that, Sheriff. Besides, you said by sundown, an' I was. But I don't recollect you say anythin' about not comin' back.'

Turgoose's look hardened dangerously. 'Don't go playin' games with me boy. You know exactly what I meant.'

Jesse shrugged. 'Yeah, I thought I did. Anyways, I'm here on business, not to go breakin' any o' your town ordinance.'

Turgoose shook his head. 'Wickett ain't doin' business today,' he said briskly.

Jesse smiled a bit, then nodded. 'Funny, Sheriff. Real funny. But I got to see Morgan Samwell, an' it won't wait until you decide the town's open.'

'What do you want with an attorney?'

'You know that's between me an' him.'

Turgoose grimaced, showed a big set of teeth. 'I ain't goin' to keep tellin' you. You either tell me so's I decide, or you ride away right now,' he commanded.

'The next time one o' them playhouses hits town, Sheriff, you climb up on stage. You'd bring the house down with your funnin',' Jesse answered back. Then he looked around him, was aware of the people gathering around, pressing closer so they didn't miss anything.

Turgoose started to get edgy, didn't want to be made fun of. 'All right, Jesse, that's enough,' he decided.

The sheriff's right arm was slightly bent, his hand hovering only inches from the butt of his Colt. Jesse stood very still. He knew that gunplay was the sheriff's next move. Having backed himself into a corner, it was his only option.

As expected, Turgoose shifted for his gun, but he'd barely moved before he stopped and his expression froze.

There was a gasp from the crowd, and most of them pressed back instinctively. Jesse was holding his own actioned Colt, and it was pointed at the sheriff's midriff. His face remained impassive.

'I've got someone to see, Sheriff,' he told the lawman quietly but firmly. 'I've not brought you any trouble, an' I want to keep it that way. What you've got here, you've brought on yourself. Now, I'm stayin' here long enough to get done what I've got to. What do you say?'

Turgoose's face was getting paler and alarm was now showing in his eyes. But there was anger too, and he swallowed hard. Some onlookers thought his right arm trembled, that he only just managed to stop himself from drawing his Colt. At the same time, Jesse thought it was because the man wasn't stupid.

'Don't threaten me on my own street, Jesse,' the man grated, his breathing now rough-edged and shallow.

'Goddamn it, John. I just told you, I *am* goin' to see Samwell. Are you goin' to try an' shoot me for it?'

Turgoose let his hand drop to his side, pressed his palm against the butt of his Colt. 'You got an hour,' he said in a strangled sort of voice.

Jesse nodded. 'Fair enough,' he said in an attempt to give the sheriff back some credibility. 'Should be all I need.'

Turgoose drew a deep breath and returned the assent. 'Yeah, well, I ain't a vindictive man. Just got me a town to protect.'

Jesse was prepared to leave him with the last word, and he smiled acceptingly as the sheriff pushed back through the small crowd. Jesse slowly holstered his Colt and turned to Morgan Samwell's office.

The attorney at law had a secretary and a clerk who wrote transcribed legal documents. The room had been much improved and refurnished since Jesse had last seen it. But he saw straightaway it still contained the big, New York safe with highly wrought decoration across its front.

The secretary looked up helpfully as Jesse pushed the door to, behind him.

'Unfortunately, Mr Samwell's not seein' anyone without an appointment,' she said, attempting to conceal a fascinated smile.

'I'm the Governor o' Texas. I'm sure he'll find some time for me,' Jesse said, and returned what he thought was a similar look.

The girl shook her head. 'I know who you are . . . an' you still can't see him.'

'Make me one, then.'

'I beg your pardon.'

'Make me an appointment. Any time will do, but as you probably know what just happened in the street, preferably sometime in the next hour.'

'That really makes no difference. Mr Samwell is fully booked for the whole day.'

Jesse nodded towards the frosted, glass-panelled door. 'Has he got some-one with him right now?'

'No, but there's someone due any moment. An' where do you think you're goin'?' she said, as Jesse moved forward.

The secretary got to her feet and stepped quickly between Jesse and the door. Jesse grinned and held up a restraining hand. 'He ain't worth dyin' for, girl. Go back to your desk an' carry on with whatever important work you were doin',' he said. 'I'll explain that you laid your life on the line tryin' to stop me.'

Not very likely, Jesse thought to himself, as he opened the door to Attorney Samwell's office.

The man had put on some weight. That was Jesse's first impression as he saw the attorney sitting behind an enormous desk. The other furniture was of an affluent style, included a wide cabinet with an striking array of decanters and glasses. Morgan Samwell had been struggling to make his name when Jesse had quit Wickett, now it looked like the man was well established. Samwell was once slight, but now he carried the sort of bulk that came with good living. He didn't look entirely out of shape, but his jaw line sagged when he recognized Jesse.

'Hello, Morg,' Jesse said. He sat casually in a leather upholstered chair, hung his hat on his bent knee and took out his Bull Durham. 'Let's pretend we're ol' friends, who've got some business goin',' he suggested.

Samwell glanced at the glass panel in his door, then frowned slightly. 'You're not in my appointment book, Jesse,' he said.

Jesse gave an amused smile as he built his cigarette. 'I know. But don't blame that girl o' yours . . . your look-out. She did try an' stop me, but I don't have a lot o' time.' He lit his cigarette and looked at Samwell through the first puff of smoke.

Samwell cleared his throat and consulted a silver, pocket watch. 'Maybe I've got a few minutes . . . under the circumstances.'

'That's good, Morg. It's what I hoped you'd say. I'm also curious as to what you mean by *circumstances*.'

Again, Samwell cleared his throat. 'Well, it is to do with the legacy your father left you, isn't it?'

Jesse just watched the man while he took a long draw on his cigarette. The man looked away, eased back in his chair and ran a finger around the inside of his collar.

'Yeah, that's right, Morg. Owen told me it's five hundred dollars.'

'That's right. It doesn't sound much, but that's down to more o' those circumstances.

'Explain,' Jesse said.

'Your father changed his will soon after you left town. Up until that time he had intended for you and Owen to share the ranch *equally*.'

Samwell braced himself as Jesse suddenly looked concerned.

'My pa was goin' to leave me half?' Jesse asked incredulously. 'Half the spread?'

'Originally, yes. But as I said, he changed — '

Jesse waved Samwell's words away.

'Yeah, I know. I want to think a moment,' he said. That fact that Festus Tripp had changed his mind didn't much interest Jesse: it's what he'd understood and come to terms with. But learning that the old man had at one time considered leaving him half the ranch, surprised him greatly. If there had been something between him and his pa, he'd missed it, but maybe there was a new slant on the way he thought about his future prospects.

Samwell started to fiddle with a small penknife. 'I guess your leavin' upset him quite a bit . . . more than you knew,' he suggested. 'He really wasn't goin' to leave you a plugged nickel. I'd like to think it was my advice that made him think different.'

'Yeah, thanks,' Jesse said almost absentmindedly as he looked around the office. 'Seems *you* done all right here, Morg. This wasn't more'n a space with a filin' cabinet, as I recall.'

'We all have to start somewhere,' Samwell protested mildly. 'There was a lot of land dealin' not long after you left. Place sort o' went crazy. Changes of title and so on ... boundary disputes. The country's growin' fast, Jesse, an' I'm goin' along with it.'

Jesse looked at him shrewdly. 'That fast growin' includes my brother?'

Samwell shifted his gaze away from Jesse. 'Yes. Owen was involved in considerable land dealin'. It was after your father met with his accident, of course.'

'Sure. But what about Billy Hugh's place? That was a clear-cut land deal, was it?'

Samwell was still uncomfortable and he glanced once again at the door. 'As I recall, I did a search for kinfolk, but there weren't any,' he answered. 'But I managed to get clear title, eventually. That meant the land could go to Triple T.'

'Well, it don't sound like the way the old man went about things,' Jesse said. 'An' why'd he want the Hugh spread. He'd more or less already got the best land in the county.'

Samwell was sweating now, but he shrugged and made a helpless gesture. 'Like most of us, I just do what I'm paid to do, Jesse. As long as it's legal, I don't ask folks their reasons for doin' things.'

Jesse's eyes were cold. 'You got a copy o' the will, here?'

The attorney grimaced and began toying with the pen-knife again. 'Well, not where I can lay my hands on it. There'll be a copy somewhere in the files, but I'd have to initiate a search. Now, if you'd had an appointment — '

Jesse stopped Samwell mid-sentence and got to his feet. 'What do you mean, 'initiate a search'? Just get up an' look for it, goddamnit,' he rasped. 'I want to see a copy o' the old will an' the new one.'

'OK, I can do that, Jesse,' Samwell agreed quickly. 'But tell me what it is you're lookin' for,' he added.

Jesse leaned across the desk and offered the attorney a mean grin. 'As long as it's legal, you don't bother with folks' reasons. Right?' he said.

Samwell swallowed and gave a sickly smile. 'Of course. I just thought maybe I could help . . . wondered if everythin' was all right.'

'I'll tell you when I see the documents. I'll give you an hour after sundown to find 'em. I reckon you owe the Tripp family that, if not me personally,' Jesse instructed the attorney. 'Meantime, let me have somethin' so's I can collect that five hundred from the bank.'

Samwell wrote a bank cheque, then added a weak, tentative signature. His hands were actually shaking, and a drop of perspiration fell and smudged the ink.

'As significant as blood,' Jesse remarked. He had a quick look at the paper, nodded, said thanks and left without another word.

Within moments of him leaving, Samwell's door opened and the anxious secretary came flustering in.

'I'm sorry, Mr Samwell, he just came right on in,' she said.

'I know. Don't worry about it. The man's trouble,' he responded, while continuing to write briskly. 'Now, I want you to find someone reliable, and get them to take this note to Triple T. I want it delivered by hand to Owen Tripp . . . no one else . . . an' as soon as possible. There's five dollars if they get there an' back before sundown.'

Samwell waved the note to dry the ink, then he folded it into an envelope which he sealed securely.

'By hand,' he repeated, 'and to no one else but Owen Tripp.'

12

Gus Tawfey was stacking coffee cans beneath the counter of his grub house, when Jesse came through the door.

'Whoa, you come to chop me up, Jesse?' he asked with a little concern.

'I suppose you still got Lupin workin' out back,' Jesse said, as he went for the fly-curtain that led to the kitchen.

'Just go on in, why don't you?' the man said. 'But you won't find her there.'

'Where is she?'

'I gave her three hours off against workin' two tonight. I ain't the slaver you seem to think.'

'Yes you are, you miserable, cheap, meat peddler,' Jesse rasped back.

'I was the one who gave her a job when she needed it. Just remember that,' Tawfey said, huffily.

'So where's she livin'?' Jesse asked.

Tawfey was silent for a moment as though considering whether to tell Jesse the address or not. 'Edge o' town, east side. You can't miss it,' he said as Jesse took a step towards him. 'A blind feller would get there easy enough.'

★   ★   ★

'Judas Priest,' Jesse cursed when he saw that Lupin's place was just as Tawfey had implied. It was a low built shack, walled with gappy planks that were chinked with scraps of rolled rag. The chimney had partly collapsed, and earth-filled gunny-sacks had been wedged into the slanting roof where shingles were missing. There had been some attempt to cultivate a strip for what looked like beans and peas, but it all looked wretched to Jesse as he rattled the door latch. 'Makes you realize how handy a feller can be,' he muttered sadly.

Lupin was very surprised to see him, and looked uncomfortable when she asked him in. He glanced around the

112

hovel, pretended not to be affected by the makeshift contents. But it was all clean, and one corner of the single room was brightened by two Navajo blankets that were nailed to the walls. He walked across to the rush cot and gently pulled the coverlet away from the child's face. 'Looks like you got yourself one crop that'll never fail,' he said, turning away with a smile. 'An' I reckon he favours you.'

Lupin returned the smile. 'I've got some coffee going if you'd like,' she offered.

'Not right now, thank you, Lupin. I came to talk about somethin' particular if it won't wake the little 'un.'

Lupin shook her head and sat in one of two rickety chairs.

'No. He'd sleep through one o' those blue whistlers. Besides, he's used to my voice.'

'Hope I don't break this,' Jesse said as he pulled the other chair near.

Lupin saw Jesse shift his jaw when he sat down and turned to face her.

'What's wrong with your neck?' she asked.

'Nothin' much. I must've been sittin' in a draught.'

'Hmm. Does John Turgoose know you're here . . . here in town?' she asked with a fretful look.

'Him an' me came to an understandin'.' Jesse saw by Lupin's expression that she expected more, but he didn't give it. Instead, he reached inside his shirt and brought out a flat package. 'I brought you this,' he said, handing it over. 'Call it an early Christmas present.'

Lupin smiled uncertainly as she slid the string free of the heavy brown paper. Then she caught her breath as she saw what had been wrapped up. 'This is money, Jesse. All money,' she said staring at the contents. 'What's it for?'

'I just told you,' Jesse told her evenly. 'I *was* thinkin' for Mano, but maybe it's best if you go shares.'

'There must be many hundreds of dollars here.'

'Yeah, five.'

Lupin shook her head rapidly. 'I can't take all this,' she said, and made to hand the package back. But Jesse stopped her, looked sternly into her confused eyes.

'Triple T treated you badly, Lupin. The whole damn town did. With this, you can thumb your nose at 'em. Just think o' the fun in that, if nothin' else.'

'I can't, Jesse.'

'Yeah, you can. It's a sort o' key stone. You can get a nice job . . . live somewhere that don't bite back. I hear they've got a Nob Hill up in Albuquerque.'

Lupin had a more thoughtful look at the wad of notes. 'Five hundred dollars,' she muttered. 'If you want me to have this money, Jesse, I want to know where you got it.'

'My pa left it to me. It's mine, all legal like. I can easy afford five hundred,' he lied.

'After all that I did . . . letting people think that . . . ?' Lupin's teeth suddenly bit into her bottom lip. 'Can you see

'. . . understand how very bad this makes me feel?'

'Yep, I can a bit. So, I'm givin' you the chance to put things right by takin' it. To me, it's a sort o' salvation for all you done wrong.'

'Mmm,' Lupin doubted, and gave Jesse a real quizzical look. 'I'm not sure. I think you're ribbing me like you used to.'

'Well, whatever, Lupin. But just take it, will you? If you keep on arguin' you'll wake the kid for certain.'

Lupin stood up and placed her free hand on Jesse's shoulder. 'I'm not going to win, am I?'

Jesse shook his head and smiled.

'And now you're going away again?'

'Chances are,' Jesse agreed. 'But I've still got to see Morgan Samwell. I'll decide later tonight,' he added.

'What's wrong, Jesse?' Lupin asked, with a sudden sense of some other problem.

'I don't know. I don't seem to know diddly squat anymore, Lupin. There's somethin' goin' on . . . maybe some-thin' that's already happened.'

Lupin seemed uncomfortable with Jesse's response. She smiled weakly and squeezed his arm. 'I'm sure everything's as it seems, Jesse. I wouldn't like to see you in more trouble. Please don't go looking for it.'

Jesse gave a faltering laugh. 'No, I won't. I can get enough o' that by just sittin' my saddle, mindin' time,' he said with heavy irony.

Lupin lifted to her toes and kissed him. Then she touched the fresh burn on his neck. 'What sort of draught was it caused *that*?' she wanted to know.

'Someone took a pot shot at me. They were in the timber up near Cottonwood Creek. But that's not for you to worry about. Come the mornin', put that money somewhere safe, have a word with Tawfey, then send off for one o' them wish books. Now I got to go see the man I was tellin' you about.'

When Jesse was gone, Lupin pulled the cover back up around Mano's chin, then sat down again. She held the sizeable bundle of money in her hands, sighed unhappily because she thought there was something she should have said.

Meanwhile, Jesse made for the Wickett Saloon. He figured on having a quiet drink or two — kill some time before his appointment with the attorney.

He was walking along the boardwalk, had just passed John Turgoose's law office when he heard the door open behind him. He paused, was immediately seized with dread at the sound of a gun hammer being cocked. Instinct made him turn, but his hand was stayed when he found himself looking into the black tunnel of the sheriff's shotgun.

Turgoose smiled deviously as he levelled the revolving gun at Jesse's chest. 'Maybe you're thinkin', he won't hit wind with that dangerous piece o' circus junk. But what you got to ask yourself is, could this be when all four barrels go off at once? If I was you, Jesse, I'd lift them hands nice an' slow.'

Beyond Turgoose stood a figure wearing a bashed up prairie hat, and a twill jacket above trousers that fell well short of a proper length. He was a rangy man, covered with trail dust, and his eyes were red raw from long days of riding.

Jesse cursed passionately, lurched with nervous tension as he recognized the dirt farmer who owned the claybank.

13

As the cell door clanged shut behind Jesse Tripp, the sheriff made a tuneless whistle as he noisily turned the key in the lock.

'I never had a real good look,' the dirt farmer was saying. 'But it sort o' looks like him.'

'It's him all right,' Turgoose assured him. 'You identified your claybank, Mr Croker, an' it's the mount he's been forkin' ever since ridin' into town.'

The man, Croker shook his head slowly. 'I figured I'd lost that horse for good. I never thought I'd get further'n reportin' it stole. Yessir, it's a real slice o' luck.'

From his cell, Jesse scowled, directed himself loudly at the two men. 'I bought that horse from a reputable trader in Toya. My own mount had shattered a knee, an' this feller had the claybank with a spare saddle. *That's* what you call a real slice o' luck.'

'Big wind's what it is,' Turgoose cut in. 'You should've took my advice, Jesse. You'd have been long gone before Croker here showed. Now you're in it up to your baby blues waitin' for the circuit judge.'

Jesse smiled cynically, shrugged and moved across to the low bunk.

'This time, you're gettin' the book thrown at you,' Turgoose continued. 'You'll be doin' time on a salt lake chain gang, an' it's your own goddamn fault.'

'How about my claybank, Sheriff?' the rancher asked anxiously. 'Can I take it back now?'

'No, 'fraid not, Mr Croker,' Turgoose replied. 'We'll need it for evidence. The hostler confirms it's the mount that Tripp rode into town on, even intimated you'd be turnin' up. So you best stick around.'

'Hell, Sheriff, I got me a wife back in the hills, an' I've already been gone over a week. Besides, I ain't got any money.'

'The county'll find for you, Mr Croker. You can stay full board in town lodgin's for a couple o' days.'

Croker sniffed out a noise in agreement, as Turgoose led them back to the front office.

Jesse sat down on his bunk, his expression, bleak. It looked like this time Turgoose really was set on taking him. Once again, he cursed at having allowed himself to be driven back to Wickett. But hell, wasn't it worth it, just to see the changing looks on Lupin's face? If anyone found out what he'd done, though, there wouldn't be much uncertainty among them about who was Mano's father. Huh, one life starts as another's just about to close down, he thought gloomily.

Less than an hour later, John Turgoose stomped back to the cell. As he jammed the key angrily into the lock, Jesse sat up in anticipation.

'Get your lyin' hide out o' there,' Turgoose commanded. 'An' don't take all goddamn day.'

But Jesse remained seated. 'I hope this ain't your '*horse thief gets shot breakin' jail*' headline for the *Gazette*,' he said.

'If you don't get up, I'll shoot you right there,' the lawman snapped.

Jesse got to his feet, snatched up his hat and strode into the passage where Turgoose glared at him.

'Croker's gone, an' charges have been dropped,' he grated. 'Seems that a bill o' sale's suddenly been found for that claybank. I should lock *him* up for causin' so much trouble.'

Jesse was still bewildered as he signed for his belongings and buckled on his gunbelt. He was going to say something about not looking a gift horse in the mouth, but guessed Turgoose wouldn't appreciate it. He just wished he knew what was going on.

'Get out o' my town, Jesse,' the lawman growled. 'I mean it this time. I want you gone.'

'Give me till seven o'clock. I promise

I'll be gone by eight.'

'Yeah? Why should I believe that.'

'Got me a little legal business to attend to. You know how Morgan Samwell's a stickler for time.'

Turgoose shook his head as an unhelpful reply.

'Seven or eight, Sheriff,' Jesse rasped. 'Please don't push for trouble,' he warned, as he slammed the door behind him. 'It won't be worth it.'

Up at the saloon bar, Brent Marler drew him a beer and indicated a near table. It was where the farmer was sitting in on a poker game. He had a bottle of house whiskey at his elbow, and he flinched when Jesse dropped a hand on his bony shoulder.

'Well, if it ain't my ol' friend Mr Croker,' Jesse said. 'I thought I heard you tellin' the sheriff, you didn't have any money.'

'Well things changed,' Croker said warily. 'No hard feelin's, I hope.'

Jesse allowed the man a thoughtful moment. 'Maybe if I knew what was goin' on, I'd know about that,' he said.

'It's the Mex who's got the bill o' sale,' Croker responded quickly, obviously trying to avoid any trouble.

'What Mex?' Jesse asked.

'The girl with the kid. She bought the claybank an' saddle . . . gave me an extra dollar to back-date the bill o' sale.'

* * *

Jesse caught up with Lupin just as she was leaving her cabin.

'What the hell are you playin' at, Lupin?' he demanded.

Lupin held a finger to her lips. 'Shhh. You want everyone to hear you? Walk with me back into town,' she replied.

Jesse matched her brisk walk, and his temper was still strong. 'Goddamn it, that money was for you and Mano,' he said.

'Yes, and I've still got most of it left. Do you *know* the going rate for a claybank mare an' saddle? Right this moment, it seems to me as if the money could serve *you* better, Jesse. I've got a bill of sale here, that says you're not a horse-thief.'

Obviously still disgruntled, Jesse took the paper. 'Yeah, I know. I'm sorry, Lupin, but I meant it *all* for you. I've got out o' that sort o' fix before.' He stopped short, and took her shoulders between his hands. Then, and unmindful of folk along the street, he leaned down and kissed her. 'More shame and disgrace,' he said and grinned. 'But why are you goin' to Tawfey's?' he asked. 'You're supposed to be findin' an alternative job, an' it doesn't have to be in Wickett, either.'

Lupin nodded. 'I know that too, Jesse. But no matter how he treats me, or how little he pays, he was the only one who'd give me work. I owe him a week's notice, at least.'

'So maybe I'll call in an' see you when I leave,' he said, admiring her steadfastness. But as he moved off, she called him.

'There's something else, Jesse. I

didn't know whether to tell you or not . . . maybe I still don't. It's because I know there'll be trouble, and — '

'Out with it Lupin. What's got you sparked?'

Lupin took a deep breath, glanced around to make sure there was no one within earshot. 'I wasn't fired from Triple T until some time after you'd gone. It was only when it showed. I always got along well enough with your father. He wasn't one for saying much, but I do know that he missed you very much.'

'I already knew most o' that, Lupin,' Jesse said. 'Christ, most of it's local bar talk. An' he couldn't have missed me more than five hundred dollars' worth. Ah,' he added quickly, then cursed for the slip of his tongue.'

'That's how much he left you? An' you gave me *all* of it?' The astonishment was plain on Lupin's face and in her voice.

'Yeah, well, I wouldn't have done if it had been any more,' Jesse retorted with mock indignity. 'An' let's not forget you've already given half of it back.'

'It wasn't half,' Lupin muttered, and shook her head, not knowing what more to say.

'So what else do you know . . . want to tell me?' Jesse continued. 'Do you know anythin' about the accident?'

Lupin took a moment to reply. 'I know that the night before your father died, there was a big argument between him an' your brother. I heard it. Most of us did,' she said.

'Yeah, this is more like it,' Jesse said. 'I was wonderin' when Owen would figure. What was the root of it . . . the argument?'

'Owen had taken over a homesteader's place — the Jukes', I think — but your pa didn't like the way he did it. They must've argued for most of the night, because your pa was still angry at breakfast. He told Owen he didn't hold with such methods. He said he'd warned him before, that this was the last time. He said, if he couldn't run a ranch properly, or honestly, then he

128

didn't deserve a share in Triple T.'

Jesse was incredulous. 'You heard my pa threaten to cut Owen from his will? You actually heard him?'

'Yes. More than me heard him.'

'Did you see or hear anythin' more?'

'I know they were still arguing when they rode off, later.'

'Did you see where they were headed?'

'West. The start of the high trail.'

'Yeah, to Buzzard Point. Go on, Lupin.'

Lupin touched her bottom lip with her fingertips while she thought. 'After, when your father's body was found, Owen said he *didn't* ride the high trail that day,' she continued quietly. 'He said your father had gone up there alone.'

'But you know different, Lupin?'

'Yes. And so does Luke Bogan. But he said he'd ridden up on Owen and your father when they were on the flats. He said he'd got Owen to go with *him*.'

Muscles knotted along Jesse's jaw line as he ground his teeth. 'You know what you're sayin', Lupin . . . what that means?'

Lupin nodded strongly when she thought Jesse might have trouble with what she'd told him. 'I'm telling you what I saw, and I've tied no weight to it, Jesse,' she replied. 'But I decided you've a right to know the truth . . . perhaps to know you've been cheated. I hope I haven't done too much wrong in telling you.'

'No, Lupin, you haven't. I had it in my mind you were goin' to tell me somethin' different. I take it no one else knows all this?'

'No. One of the kitchen girls heard the argument. But I think that's all. And I didn't know who or what to tell. I didn't even realize what it all meant, until much later, and I had my own worries by the time Owen fired me.'

'Why'd you decide to tell me now, Lupin?' Jesse asked.

'You saying your father had only left you five hundred dollars. Something grated.'

'Yeah, ain't that the truth. Well, I'll soon goddamn find out *what*,' Jesse returned.

Now the sun had gone down and deep shadows were filling the town. Jesse was suddenly concerned about the increasing darkness, but it was too risky for a gunman to be lurking, hidden or otherwise, and he shook the thought away.

'I've got to get somethin' from Morgan Samwell, and then I'll go an' see Owen,' he said.

'You be real careful, Jesse. In this town, trouble usually depends on whether you're coming or going. I think maybe that's another reason I was slow to tell you.'

'That's real smart, Lupin. Agreeable, too. Anythin' you ever feel you owed me's now fully paid.' Jesse then had a furtive look around him. 'I'll walk you to Tawfey's,' he said, and smiled.

14

Gus Tawfey was standing on the boardwalk in front of the grub house door. For a moment, as he emerged from the gloom, Jesse imagined he saw the hint of an intolerant scowl on the man's face — perhaps a sentiment he would have saved for Lupin if she'd been on her own.

'This ain't the time we agreed, an' there's hungry fellers inside,' Tawfey said, looking towards Lupin. 'You'd better trip lively.'

Jesse assumed Tawfey's foolhardiness must be a joke, so he smiled. 'Yeah, she's takin' advantage, just 'cause she's got me along,' he answered back, smiled wryly at Lupin as she went on past him.

'*Adios*, kid, an' thanks,' he said, as she returned the smile.

Still muttering, Tawfey turned to

follow Lupin inside, but Jesse moved quickly behind him and prodded him hard in the shoulder. 'Hey, you fat grease ball. I already told you, to go easy on the girl. That's somethin' you forget at your peril,' he warned him.

A few minutes later and further down the street, Jesse saw the lights go out in Morgan Samwell's office. 'Don't you go closin' up yet, Morg,' he said, and broke into a loping run.

Drawing close, just about to leap on to the boardwalk, he faltered at the loud, hollow-sounding bang. He instinctively knew it was a gunshot from inside the attorney's office.

'Aagh, no,' he said and pulled his Colt. The street door to the office was closed and the interior was in total darkness. In the immediate dead silence that followed the gun crash, he stood very still, listening, thinking how to go in. Then, from the side alley at the side of the office he heard a window sliding up in its frame. He took three steps, and eased around the corner, watched intently as a dark form unbent through the opened window and dropped to the ground.

'Hey, gotcha,' he grated. 'Hold up there, feller, don't try an' run,' he charged. But the drop was more than six feet and the man landed heavily and off balance. His legs buckled with the impact and he stumbled in the dirt, fired off another shot as he turned and stumbled deeper into the alley.

Jesse drew himself away. Then he took a deep breath, went down on one knee and eased back around the corner. Almost immediately, another shot chewed into the wood above his head and he cursed, twisted quickly back again.

In the darkness of the narrow passageway, the gunman gained his feet and started to run. Jesse jumped down from the boardwalk, and holding his Colt firmly in front of him, he fired off two rounds. The man ahead turned to take another shot, but Jesse stood firm, returned fire with two more measured shots.

Jesse heard the man grunt, dimly saw him stagger, almost go down. Then the man was gone, disappeared around a corner as Jesse fired again. Jesse ran forward, flattened himself against a clapboard wall before edging around it, warily. Next thing, he heard galloping hoofs, guessed the rider would be emerging somewhere along the main street. Knowing he'd never get close enough to give chase, he cursed, deciding to check on Samwell, ran back down the alley.

He became aware of the commotion in the street ahead of him. 'Christ, if this don't bring the town out, nothing will. Where are you, Turgoose?' he said.

As he drew level with the open window of Samwell's office, he jumped and pulled himself up and over the sill, climbed through the window. 'If you're alive in here, don't shoot. I've come to help,' he called out in desperation.

Then he saw the dark shape lying on the floor beside the big desk. He knelt to feel a still warm body, but wasn't sure if the man was dead or still breathing. He found the desk lamp and the vesta box, waited a moment while the yellow light spilled over the sprawled body. Morgan Samwell was staring up at his office ceiling with glazed, distant eyes. There was a dark patch on his expensive silk shirt and his chest heaved shallow.

Jesse knelt beside him. 'Morg, it's Jesse . . . Jesse Tripp. Who was it shot you?'

Jesse put his head close, but the attorney made no sound. Blood trickled from a corner of his mouth, and he just stared up at him. There was no flicker of movement until he closed his eyes to die.

Jesse stood up and leaned against the desk, stayed there a full minute until the front door opened and John Turgoose moved across the threshold. Close behind, Samwell's secretary craned to see beyond the man's shoulder. Her eyes widened and she placed her knuckles in her mouth to partly stifle a gasp.

Turgoose levelled an icy stare at Jesse. 'So, this is the little bit o' legal business you had to attend to, is it?'

'Don't talk rubbish, Sheriff. I was comin' to see him when I heard a shot. Whoever did it, climbed out o' the window I just climbed in. You must have heard what was happenin'. Who'd you think I was tradin' lead with in the alley . . . a goddamn spook? He had a horse waitin' out back somewhere, but I think I hit him.'

Samwell's secretary pushed around Turgoose, pointed a tremulous finger at Jesse. 'That's him, Jesse Tripp,' she said. 'He came in here this afternoon, all proddy like. I tried to stop him . . . I heard him threaten Mr Samwell.'

'What did he say?' the sheriff asked.

'He told Mr Samwell to get him his father's will. Said it would be the worst for him, if he didn't.'

'I never threatened him,' Jesse retorted. 'I didn't have to. I told him he owed it to the Tripp family.'

'An' later you put a bullet in him,'

137

Turgoose stated crudely and swung up the barrel of his shotgun. 'Put your Colt on the desk, Jesse. An' real delicate like,' he commanded.

A few concerned men were now crowding into the office and around the window, and Jesse hesitated. But he knew there was no way out, and he laid his gun carefully on the desk, stepped back at a gesture from Turgoose's gun barrel.

'This time, I aim to keep you locked up for more'n a couple of hours. Let's go home,' the sheriff grated. Then he picked up the Navy Colt and rammed it into his own belt.

Jesse smiled thinly, shook his head in exasperation. 'While you're makin' one more hell of a big mistake with me, Sheriff, the real killer's hightailin' it for the Blancas, or back to whatever ranch he slithered out of,' he rasped.

The mood of the crowd was now edgy, getting intolerant. They wanted something done, and Turgoose prodded Jesse forward. The secretary suddenly took a step forward, caught Jesse a stinging blow across his face.

'I hope you rot in hell for what you did,' she hissed.

Jesse winced, rubbed a hand across his cheek. Defying Turgoose's gun, he glared back at the girl. 'You'd know where my father's will is,' he accused. 'See if you can find it.'

Indifferently, the girl lifted one or two papers off Samwell's desk. She looked down into the paper bin, shook her head at the sheriff.

'If it was like he says, it would be here. It's not,' she said.

'It ain't the sort o' document that gets thrown in the bin. Look in the goddamn safe, why don't you?' Jesse snorted.

'Just take him away, Sheriff,' she said to Turgoose.

His patience exhausted, Turgoose shoved Jesse from the office. 'Now we do what I want, an' that's gettin' you back behind bars. That ol' bunk might still have some warmth in it. An' one o' you good folk see to it that Mr Samwell gets attended to,' he added, sharply.

'It was the gunman who took the papers. He took a bullet, so you should be able to find him,' Jesse muttered, and walked from the office without further argument.

15

When he was under lock and key again, Jesse vainly tried Lupin's story on the sheriff. But Turgoose's response was predictable. He had looked into the story, found that it was highly probable that Festus Tripp's horse had shied at a rattlesnake. He'd likely then fallen from the saddle, and over the point. The lawman wasn't interested in any other speculation and he'd decided to close the case.

'An' with a fair wind, I'll wrap this one up in a few days,' he stated. 'Do you realize that for killin' Morgan Samwell, you've gone from breakin' rocks along the Brazos, to havin' your neck stretched in El Paso?' he concluded. 'Sleep tight, feller, get used to the long one.'

Hours later, lying on the coarse bedding in the dark cell, Jesse tried to figure out who it was he'd seen climbing from Samwell's office window. There hadn't been enough light for him to discern any distinctive features, but he knew it wasn't anyone weighty or short on stature.

He grinned sardonically in the darkness. In fact, if anyone had been asked to describe who they'd seen, they'd describe Jesse Tripp to a T. He was so prime suspect, there wasn't any real need for a trial. No, that's enough, he thought, stop this goddamn nightmare.

However, he then got to thinking about who wanted to stop him seeing the wills, when the only person who could possibly benefit would be his brother.

He cursed again, considered the motives. Maybe the old man *had* been thrown from his horse. Maybe Owen knew, but used it to his own advantage. The reasons whirled around until Jesse felt a grip of certainty. Owen had always claimed he operated in Jesse's shadow. He had all the hard chores in and around the ranch while Jesse rebelled against just about everything, including their father. Perhaps understandably, Owen reasoned he was entitled to inherit Triple T. That was one thing, though. Being jealous enough to kill was something else, Jesse decided, and took another fork in his road of thinking. He decided that the old man's death must have been an accident. If Owen had been there, he wouldn't have stood by and not helped. But knowing that others had heard him and his pa arguing, he probably would have panicked. Then he would have been afraid of how it had looked, so he talked Luke Bogan into giving him an alibi, got him to swear he was miles away when the old man had died. If Owen had done that, he'd certainly have promised Bogan something in return.

Jesse took a long breath, continued with his string of thoughts. It was Festus leaving *equal* shares that had got to Owen, and could be the will had never been changed. Owen was on

Buzzard Point all right, but it wasn't so much as what he'd done up there, as hadn't done.

More'n one way to skin a cat, eh, Owen? Jesse reflected. For himself, he was a firebrand, and already riding the owl-hoot trail. No one much expected to see him again, certainly not around Wickett or Triple T.

'Just as well I ain't on the loose, Sheriff,' he called out. 'In here you got time to make sense . . . get things sorted.'

For a few more uncomfortable minutes, Jesse got back to firming up his thoughts. Maybe Owen had then come to an arrangement with his attorney. Morgan Samwell always claimed the law had to be resourceful. There was a printed motto hanging opposite his desk that read: *The law's a flexible tool. Sometimes you make it bend one way, sometimes the other.*

Samwell had said the country was going crazy with land deals, and he was going along with it. Yeah, and Triple T had doubled in size. Owen would've thrown plenty of business Samwell's way, and Samwell would've kept quiet about Jesse's share of the ranch. And just in case Jesse did return, they would fob him off with a £500 gift.

But Morgan Samwell was the flaw. For Owen, there was a lot at stake — a lot to lose — and Jesse's young brother certainly had enough money to pay someone to take care of any such things.

'Hey, Sheriff. I know who you should put in here instead o' me,' Jesse shouted. 'Yeah, I thought you'd be interested,' he added, after a few seconds of silence.

Jesse had no idea of the time, but now the twisted feeling in his belly became the growl of hunger. He got up, went over and pressed the side of his face against the bars, saw there was no band of light under the door at the end of the dark passage.

If it is you, Owen, you'll be wantin' me dead. If a jury finds me guilty — which is a goddamn certainty — your future's safe. But you have to live with it, Brother, an' sleep at night, were Jesse's concluded thoughts.

Turgoose had made Jesse empty his pockets before locking him in his cell. The only metal he had was his brass belt buckle. He used the tongue to probe the interior of the lock, but it was too short, not firm enough to move the sturdy spring away from its tumblers.

Although he knew it wouldn't do him any good, he cursed with exasperation and resentment. For another half-hour, he'd been sitting at the far end of the bunk with his head in his hands when he heard a sound at the end of the passageway. He stared into the immediate darkness until he heard the cautious drawing of a door bolt, the groan of the door swinging open. Then there was a harsh clink, then silence.

Jesse rolled silently on to the dirt-packed floor. He dragged the coarse grey blanket down with him, and pulled it around his body so that his shape would be obscured against the adobe walls. So much for being safe behind bars, he mused darkly. He was a goddamn sitting duck.

He held his breath when the key turned in the cell lock, at the sharp grate of the hinges as the door opened.

'Jesse?' the voice asked, husky and low.

Jesse let out his breath, as he recognized Lupin's voice. 'Lupin?'

'Yes. Quick, before the sheriff comes to.'

'What the hell you done? How'd you get past him?'

'Keep quiet,' she said, and held out her hand, warily lead him from the cell and along the passageway.

The front office held enough light for Jesse to see that Turgoose was sitting slumped in his chair. He was fast asleep, snoring low and deep with a bottle held in the crook of his arm.

'Most of the town knows our sheriff doesn't get around much after ten,' Lupin explained quietly. 'He's got his sleeping partner with him. Even havin' you as a prisoner, he's not changing his spots.'

The drawers of Turgoose's desk were warped, and Lupin hopped from foot to foot impatiently as, one by one, Jesse carefully pulled them open. He found his gunrig and buckled up. Then, holding his hand out for the keys, he stepped over to the sheriff's gun cabinet.

'There's no time. Your horse is saddled and in the alley,' Lupin said hurriedly.

'I need another gun,' he hissed back.

But at that moment they heard footsteps on the boardwalk outside of the law office. Jesse ushered her back towards the passageway and closed the door behind them. Cursing, he drew three heavy bolts of the door that led into the back alley and stepped down. He waited for Lupin to follow, then he pushed the door back to.

'I'll hole up by the Cottonwood Creek,' he said. 'There's a rocky outcrop, an' a ridge where the river bends. Above it, there's thick crowns o' bluestem. Do you know the place?'

'Where there's high grasses. Yes, I know where you mean.'

'From there, I'll be able to see you comin'. If you can, bring me some food. But remember Turgoose ain't no fool. You're the one he'll be watchin' because of it. *Adios* again, kid.'

Next thing, a boom of gunfire exploded from inside the jailhouse.

'Hellfire, he's set off that goddamn cannon,' Jesse shouted breathlessly. He waved at Lupin to run, then he backed off and punched three fast shots into the door as it started to open.

He heard Turgoose's curses as the man instantly slammed the door back shut.

'Somethin' raised the beast,' Jesse muttered, then turned away fast and ran for the saddled claybank. He vaulted into the saddle wheeled the mount, and kicked his heels. 'Yeah, must beat pullin' a wagon,' he said to the mount as it ran for the end of town.

Behind him, John Turgoose stepped out into the main street and started yelling. There were two more blasts from the man's revolving shotgun, but Jesse was too far off now. He lashed at the horse with the reins and kicked his heels into its flanks, drove it fast into the vast protection of darkness.

16

Owen Tripp was taking a late bourbon in his front parlour when there was an erratic knocking at the door. He looked up from his *Stockman's Journal* as the door opened, got to his feet when Luke Bogan staggered in. The man was unsteady on his feet, didn't make any effort to close the door behind him. His face was grey and beaded with sweat, and his shirt and jacket were caked with trail dust and blood. His legs buckled and he staggered across the study, tripped on the cow hide before collapsing on to a low couch. He leaned forward, stared down, blinked at the floor.

'Judas Priest,' Owen hissed hurrying over to his foreman. 'What the hell happened to you?'

Bogan raised his pain-racked face. 'Pour me somethin',' he croaked.

Owen grimaced and nodded, turned to the drinks and splashed out a liberal dose of his Kentucky bourbon. Bogan grasped the big tumbler, spilled some over his chin as he gulped down the blistering liquid. He swallowed, held his other hand low around his ribs and coughed with pain.

'Tell me what happened,' Owen demanded. 'Are you hurt? Did you get the papers?'

Bogan nodded. 'I've been hit,' he said, and pulled two envelopes from his shirt. They had once been closed by legal seals, but now the threads fixed to the flaps hung loose. Owen grabbed the envelopes, and curled his lip offensively at the smears of blood. He laid them on the end of the couch, then peeled back Bogan's jacket to see the wound.

The bullet seemed to have caught him from behind and just above his waist. Bogan had wadded his neckerchief over the wound, but it was sodden with blood and had done little to staunch the bleeding. The man's trousers were soaked dark almost to the knees.

'Who shot you? Not Samwell?' Owen asked.

Bogan rolled his head. 'No, it weren't him. But he tried to blackmail us,' he replied, with difficulty. 'Jesse had been to see him . . . like he said in his note. Morg never told us he kept your pa's real will. I had to rough him up. He was wantin' more money, even threatened to spill the beans. I had to do somethin'.'

The colour drained from Owen's face and took a couple of steps back. 'You killed him?' he breathed in disbelief.

'He was goin' to talk. Why else did he keep the real will? He was ready an' waitin' for Jesse.'

'How did *you* get shot?'

'I was just leavin' when Jesse showed up. We had a gun fight out in the alley an' he caught me. You got to get me a doc, Owen.'

'You goddamn fool,' Owen cursed his foreman. 'You were just supposed to throw a scare into him, an' bring me the wills. I wanted *them* destroyed, not the attorney.'

'You weren't there, Owen. I had to shut him up. You ain't the only one implicated.'

But Owen didn't seem to hear. He was thinking something else, staring at a point across the room. 'I don't know how far I can trust John Turgoose,' he said. 'He's out for himself, always has been. I'm thinkin' if he finds out about the wills, he could put two an' two together.'

'But he won't. We've got 'em. An' he had Jesse locked up on some horse-stealin' charge.'

'What horse-stealin' charge?'

'I don't know. Lupin got him off. She squared things with the rancher whose horse it was.'

Owen stared hard at Bogan, thought for a moment. 'With *what* did she square things?'

Once again, Bogan slowly shook his head and let out a low groan. 'It must've been Jesse gave her the money.'

Owen's look of concern increased. 'Yeah. Perhaps he figured he was good for it . . . figured he'd be gettin' his cut of Triple T.'

'Turgoose could be thinkin' it was Jesse who nailed Samwell,' Bogan suggested. 'He turned up on time, an' Turgoose ain't brimmin' with love for him.'

Owen made a crooked grin. 'Wouldn't that be dandy?' he said thoughtfully. 'Look, you'd better get out o' here. Lie low for a while.'

'If I don't get some doctorin', I'll be lyin' deep, not low.'

'It ain't much more than a flesh wound,' Owen said. 'Did the boys see you ride in?'

'No. I stayed in the timber till it was clear. No one saw me.'

'Good. We'll get you seen to, then you find somewhere up in the hills.'

'Why up there?'

'Maybe Jesse got a look at you.'

'It was dark. An' if he'd known who it was, he'd have come after me.'

'Not right away he wouldn't. There would have been a few folk who wanted an explanation. So, I don't want you around. Specially as you're wrapped around one o' Jesse's bullets.'

'You ain't bein' very accommodatin', Owen. I expected more,' Bogan suggested ominously. 'What I know could probably hang you. An' maybe your good wife would be interested in who's the real father of Lupin's kid. So in the circumstances — '

Bogan chewed on his words and his head jolted to one side as Owen backhanded him hard across the mouth. The man gasped, jerked the other way, as Owen struck him again.

Owen grabbed Bogan by the front of his shirt. 'You're in this as deep as me, you son-of-a-bitch,' he rasped with fury. 'You ever threaten me again, or breathe a word to Holly, an' I'll feed you to the goddamn snappers.'

Bogan's eyes blazed with anger. But he knew he wasn't in much of a position to argue. 'I ain't goin' up to the hills. Why can't I stay here, out o' sight?'

'I'm not takin' the risk. I'll say I sent you to Chimney Point to look for them pedigree bulls we heard about. I'll send for you in a week or so.'

Bogan made a painful, disgruntled sound. 'I'm stayin' on Triple T range,' he said, still thinking he deserved better. 'I'll go coldharbour somewhere along the Cottonwood. If you want me, send someone. I'll see 'em.'

Owen nodded. 'OK, that'll do,' he agreed. 'Now, I'll get you some provisions while Mercedes cleans an' puts a dressin' on that wound.'

Owen picked up the blood-smeared envelopes from the couch. He headed for the kitchen, didn't see the movement in the hallway outside of the parlour.

Holly had overheard most of the conversation between the two men, and she was breathing shallow with bewilderment. For a long time she'd had suspicions about the father of Lupin's child. Now, hearing Bogan's threat, the implications sickened and scared her. She was an intelligent woman, could quickly pull together the talk of old wills, even make sense of Samwell's threat of blackmail. Owen had lied about Jesse being the father of Lupin's child, so why not something else, and far worse?

'Who's that?' Owen snapped a few minutes later as Holly moved from the deep shadow.

'It's only me,' she returned, making out she'd only just got there. 'Why are you so jumpy? And where's Mercedes going with the hand basin? Is someone hurt?'

Owen stepped forward, a tight grin on his face. 'It's OK, Holly,' he said. 'Nothin' to worry about. Luke had an argument with some bobwire out on the range. I asked Mercedes to bandage him up but he needs to see the sawbones.'

'I can help,' Holly offered.

'No, no need.' Owen stepped into her

path, and shook his head. 'Mercedes can handle it. Needs a special sort o' stomach for where he's got himself hurt. You turn in, I'll be along shortly.'

'If you're sure you can manage between you,' Holly said, and looked steadily into his eyes.

'Yeah, I'm sure, Holly. You go on . . . see you in a while.' Then he turned to Mercedes, his voice toughening. 'An' we'll need some soap an' clean dressin',' he said.

Holly turned away with her heart hammering. Another lie. How many more? she wondered and swore to herself.

17

Lupin Contento felt her heart lurch when she opened the door to John Turgoose.

The lawman was red-eyed and stubbled, and the smell of horses and sweat wafted towards her. She knew immediately, the posse had returned to town and he'd come straight to her. By the look on his face, they'd been unsuccessful in their chase.

Turgoose pushed his way into the cabin, took a glance at Manolito, who was asleep in his cot.

'Jesse Tripp's loose,' he said roughly turning back towards her.

Lupin shook her head. 'I've been here all morning. Have you released him?'

Turgoose curled his lip. 'Don't get smart with me,' he warned. 'You know damn well what I mean.'

Lupin clamped her jaw tight, said nothing and tried to control her fast breathing. Then she gasped and stumbled back as Turgoose's right hand shoved her. She took a line between her and Manolito, but Turgoose was beside her instantly, hustling her to one side, away from her child.

'It was you broke him out of jail. You goddamn *puta*,' he fumed.

Lupin was afraid for Manolito and she shook her head violently. 'No,' she protested, cowering as Turgoose raised an aggressive hand. She pushed past him and lifted the child from its cot. She thought that if she faced up to the angry lawman, admitted it was her, Turgoose would take his revenge there and then. 'I don't know what you're talkin' about, Sheriff,' she told him.

'I'm talkin' about you sneakin' into my jail to bust him loose. Do you know how many friends he's got in this town? I wonder how many of 'em would've done that, knowin' he was a goddamn horse-thief?'

'I don't understand,' Lupin replied. 'What makes you think . . . ?'

'I don't need no lickerish Mex to question my thinkin,' Turgoose rasped back viciously. 'From now on, you put one foot where I don't like it, an' I'll stick you to the nearest goddamn pear. You an' that kid. You got it?'

Turgoose glowered chillingly at the child in Lupin's arms, then stormed from the cabin.

* * *

Jesse figured the last place Turgoose and his posse would look for him would be on Triple T land. But he knew that Turgoose wasn't a fool, wouldn't be deceived too easily. Once he set out to get a man, it took a lot to swerve him off the trail. Jesse smiled wryly at the thought that keeping them locked up was maybe a different matter. He knew he should be riding on, but something was still niggling about Owen. He had to find out what, at least get the truth

162

about his father's death. And Turgoose and the posse wouldn't move him before that.

During the night, he'd laid a false trail, but knew it wouldn't stand up too well in daylight. He walked the claybank upstream, rested on a patch of hard, shaley ground until sunrise. With early light to help him, he'd made a convincingly good job of covering his tracks. If they'd followed him this far, they'd likely lose him from there on.

He backtracked on the opposite bank, continued to cover his trail as he rode. He looked out across the swathes of primrose and matchweed, thoughtfully studied the landscape around him. He rode on slowly, used bankside shingle to lose his horse's prints where cattle came to drink. Eventually he recrossed the river and made for Triple T land. After another twenty minutes, he took a low, sloping rise to overlook the spot where bluestem grass clumped high on the river's rocky bank.

He tied his mount into a squat

willow, settled into position where he could watch the river and surrounding rangeland. For a short while he closed his eyes, hoped Lupin would bring him some food.

Although Jesse had taken every care to hide his trail, a lone rider sitting a distant, but parallel ridge, spotted him. Luke Bogan smirked wickedly. If he could nail Jesse Tripp now, he could claim he'd been wounded in the ensuing gunfight, could go and see the town doctor without deception. He slid a Winchester from its scabbard, grunted aloud at the pain of twisting. Then he kneed his mount forward. He wasn't giving any margin to Jesse. With a little luck, he'd never know what hit him.

★ ★ ★

Lupin had said goodbye to Manolito, and spoken to the woman who looked after him. She pulled the door of the cabin to, looked up to see a rider sitting a bay mare alongside her brush fence. It was Holly Tripp, and her face looked grim as she nodded a greeting.

'Hello, Lupin,' she said. 'I'd like a few minutes o' your time, if you please.'

'I'm on my way to work, Mrs Tripp,' Lupin replied coolly. 'If you'd like to dismount, perhaps we could walk.'

'I would prefer somewhere more private than the street,' Holly started. But Lupin was moving on, and she had no choice but to follow. She was getting piqued because it appeared she was already losing the initiative. 'I'm sorry, I would appreciate your full attention,' she said and reached out for Lupin's arm.

Lupin's eyes sparkled with annoyance, but she kept her voice level. 'It's just that Mr Tawfey gets so upset when I'm even a few minutes late.'

'I'll only keep you a few minutes. I've got a simple question, an' I'd like an honest answer,' Holly said.

Lupin met her gaze. 'If I choose to answer you, it will be. I don't lie,' she replied.

'No. Well, in this case, I hope not,' Holly said. 'Is Jesse the father o' your child?'

Lupin wasn't certain if it was the question she was expecting, and the surprise showed on her face. 'You know the answer to that, like everyone else in town,' she countered.

'Hmm, that's a clever answer, Lupin, almost as if you'd got it ready. I know you've allowed everyone to think Jesse was the father, but now I want you to tell me truth.'

Lupin hesitated, then looked directly into Holly's face. 'No Mrs Tripp,' she said, 'Jesse is not the father. He's never been with me, despite what you and the rest of the town had in mind.'

Holly bit back the retort that rose to her lips. She wanted a bit more from Lupin and didn't think she'd get it by antagonizing her.

'Then . . . ?' Holly found it impossible to stop herself from attempting the obvious question. 'You do know who?' she added unwisely and pointlessly.

Lupin's face immediately hardened. 'I think we both know the answer to that, Mrs Tripp,' she replied.

'My husband,' Holly confirmed, in a voice that was little more than a resigned whisper.

Lupin hesitated and then nodded slowly. 'It was my fault when everyone blamed Jesse. He had gone anyway, so I thought there was no harm. I actually believed it would be better if Owen was not harmed by gossip. Then it was too late to change my story and Owen threw me off the ranch.' The girl shrugged helplessly. 'I am sorry for you, Mrs Tripp. But you did ask,' she added.

Holly's face was drained of colour now, and she balled her small, gloved fists. She dragged down a deep breath and let it hiss out slowly. 'Seems we've all wronged Jesse,' she said.

'Yes,' Lupin agreed. 'But I did tell Jesse how sorry I was. He bears no grudge. But of course, that only makes me feel worse.'

'Lupin, I have to know,' Holly then

came out with. 'When you were with Owen . . . were you . . . you know . . . willing?'

Lupin thought for a moment then shook her head. 'Are you wondering if this is where the honest answers stop?' she asked, her eyes trying to read Holly. 'He didn't rape me, if that's what you mean,' was her answer.

'Then you teased him into it,' Holly said, her voice trembling.

'I guess so. I realized too late what I was doing. Maybe you shouldn't blame Owen too much,' Lupin advised with a distinct trace of deception.

Holly stopped walking and looked along the street, saw they were approaching the place where Lupin said she was working. 'What's happened to Jesse?' she asked.

Lupin studied Holly for a long moment before answering. 'I think it's best if we go back home,' she said. 'It really doesn't matter if I'm late. It doesn't matter at all.'

A short while later, Lupin hired a

horse from the livery stable. With half a gunny-sack of provisions, she took a route through the backstreets.

But Sheriff John Turgoose had been watching her for some time. When she emerged from the outskirts of the town, he was already overlooking her trail. Once clear of Wickett, Lupin increased her pace. The lawman smiled thinly, let her go almost a mile before starting after her.

18

Less than six inches from Jesse's face, the big calibre bullet smashed into the silvery, runnelled bark of the willow. He heard the report from the rifle, instinctively scrambled to the protected side of the gnarled trunk.

The claybank whinnied and reared as Jesse flung himself behind the protective timber. He drew his Colt, as the rifle's whiplash reverberated down to the course of the river, along the rocky sides and overhangs.

Then the rifle cracked out repeatedly, and a hail of lead tore through the low bending willow, sending foliage in all directions. He cursed and broke from cover, ran dipping and swerving for fifty, sixty feet before making the cutbank. Then he went to ground, rolled over the edge and down into the overhang. Dust and grit spurted from the rim, kept him from looking back and pin-pointing the rifleman.

'The last time I was anywhere near here, it weren't dodgin' bullets,' he recalled with nervous humour. The shooting had stopped momentarily and he raised his head slowly, saw a smudge of gunsmoke hanging above the distant ridge.

As he watched, the breeze broke up the hanging cloud and moved it along, but Jesse reckoned the gunman was now moving from the ridge down to the river bank. He caught a glint, guessed it was light off the man's gun barrel. He squinted to have a better look, but the rifle opened up again, spat up clumps of earth and grass in front of him. He fell back to the damp ground, cursed as the bullets chipped more stone and dirt from the lip of the overhang above. 'I'm beginnin' to think we've met before, feller,' he muttered and touched his neck with the fingers of his left hand. 'I sort o' recognize your style.'

He pulled himself up and over the

cutbank, started running back through the bluestem. Jesse's claybank was taut with nerves, remained standing near the tree with its head lowered. Jesse whacked its rump with the side of his Colt and told it to scram. 'Down stream's safer!' he yelled after it, then quickly kneeled beside the gnarled bole of the old willow. Making the clamour that Jesse wanted, the startled horse ran for where it could see cover in the distant timber.

The rifleman started shooting again, but in doing so gave away his position. Then after three more shots the firing ceased and Jesse figured it was for a reload. He leaped from his cover and ran, took the slope to try and get above the shooter.

'Goddamn it,' he yelled and fell, tripping forward. The man must have loaded swiftly, or else he'd seen Jesse and started shooting with a part-filled magazine. Bullets whipped through the long grass, and Jesse spread-eagled before rolling on to his back. As he stared into the great blue sky, the shooting stopped again, and he was up. Bent low, he ran zigzag, went for the next cover of some scattered boulders, higher up the slope.

Nearly there, he turned and saw the rifleman rise up from behind the lip of the cutbank. He watched the gun barrel search him out, cut loose with the Colt in three good, fast shots. As grit and grass blew up in front of the rifleman, Jesse made it to cover. The rifle shot went wide, and he dived between two of the boulders, twisted around on to his knees. But the man now below him had already beaded his quarry, and another short salvo of shots blasted around Jesse.

The bullets ricocheted off the boulders, but they were effective protection. Jesse leaned around one of them and snapped off another shot. The rifle fire ceased, but only for a moment. He saw the barrel of the man's gun, but knew it was firing blind. To achieve an aimed shot, the man would have to make himself a clear target.

Jesse held his Colt firmly in both hands. He eased the hammer back as he sighted along the long barrel, aimed at the precise spot he figured the man would show. A moment later he did, and Jesse pulled the trigger.

The .36 bullet struck the frame of the rifle and slewed across the ambusher's face. The gun was blasted from the man's grip as he clapped both hands to his face. Jesse was still aiming at the spot as the man staggered upright, and he fired again. 'End o' the day for you, Bogan,' Jesse rasped as lead slammed into the Triple T foreman's chest. The man rocked, then slowly went down, clawed at the rim of the cutbank before letting go and disappearing.

Jesse was up and running. With his Colt held out in front of him he made the edge of the cutbank, approached warily until he was staring down at Bogan's crumpled body. He swung himself down, knelt, and held the barrel close to the side of Bogan's bloody face.

Then he grunted, used his left hand to jerk the man's six-gun free of its holster. He tossed it out into the creek and then pushed his own Colt in the front of his pants belt. He looked at the deep gash that opened Bogan's cheek, the shirt front that was already sodden with fresh blood.

He pulled apart the man's clothing to check the wound. He thought it was close to the heart, had likely penetrated a lung. Then, lower down, he saw a fresh dressing and binding.

'You're hurt bad, Bogan, but this time, there ain't no one to patch you up,' he told the Triple T foreman.

Bogan's breathing was laboured and ragged and he didn't move for a while. But then he slowly turned his head and opened his pain-filled eyes. 'What d'you mean . . . this time?' he breathed out slowly.

Jesse smiled thinly, gestured to the bandages. 'I did this when you were leavin' Morgan Samwell's office. You came out o' the window after puttin' a bullet into him. I knew it had to be you.'

Bogan attempted a nod, but coughed painfully as thick, rising blood filled his throat.

'Yeah, smart,' he ground out. His chest felt like someone had built a fire on it. Breathing was a massive effort, and his mind wandered considerably. 'I went for the wills . . . all I wanted.'

Jesse nodded. 'That's 'cause Owen don't do his own dirty work. You ought to have known that. Did he change them?'

'Yeah,' the man said through another wave of pain. 'He faked the ol' man's signature. He'd been doin' it for years . . . never figured he got enough.'

'How about Pa's death? I know you gave Owen an alibi, but I know where he was. He was on Buzzard Point with Pa just before he died. I've got a witness.'

Bogan took so long to answer, that for a moment Jesse thought he'd breathed his last. But then the killer nodded. His eyelids fluttered, opened and his eyes flicked from side to side. He found it harder to speak his thoughts than to form them in his head, and his voice was only a grating whisper.

'He was fightin' with your pa.'

'Over what? What did they fight over?'

'The way he got hold of homesteaders' land ... them along the river bottom.'

Jesse was suddenly afraid that Bogan would die before he got the information he needed. 'How did he do it?' he demanded. 'Tell me, Bogan, an' we'll get you out o' here an' into town for some doctorin'.'

It took Bogan a little while to stop his line of thought and answer. 'He bought up their mortgages ... told bank your pa had authorized it,' he said quietly.

'Then he foreclosed an' Pa found out he'd forged everythin'. Is that what happened? Did Owen kill Pa?' Jesse gritted.

Bogan tried to move, but went into a spasm of agonized coughing. His face was grey and waxy, beaded with sweat. Blood was oozing on to his chin, covering the hollow of his throat. 'He never said as much. But I guess . . . '

Jesse knew it was near the end for Bogan. There wasn't much left to answer for. 'What's your part in it, Bogan?' he asked the dying man.

'Billy Hugh. You remember him . . . his sister? She got the spread. That's how it started . . . me gettin' hold o' the will to destroy it. Owen bought the place up for chicken feed . . . Samwell helped him . . . got all the land deals . . . made him rich. Your pa knew none of it.'

'You're all a sorry bag o' vermin,' Jesse snarled. 'Was it you took the wills from Samwell, last night?'

Bogan was growing weaker, but he managed a slight movement of his head. 'Owen's got 'em both.'

Jesse was quiet for a spell. 'An' it was you fired on me from up in the timber,' he stated.

Bogan made a quick, weak gulp. 'I'm hurtin' real bad, now. You goin' to get me back to town?' he pleaded.

'No,' Jesse said, and shook his head. 'You're goin' to die right here.'

With that Bogan stared, but he didn't see. Then he closed his eyes and let out a long, shallow breath of air, was dead within a minute.

'Now you can go to Hell,' Jesse rasped grimly.

19

Lupin Contento gasped, pulled hard on the reins when John Turgoose suddenly appeared before her. They were on the trail that led to Cottonwood Creek, and the lawman's face was drawn, tight with irritation.

As Lupin had ridden into the foothills, she'd seen a little dust about a mile behind, and it had satisfied her that her plan was working. But now her heart pounded, because she didn't know how Turgoose had got ahead of her.

'I warned you before, not to mess with me,' he snarled, nudging his horse slowly forward. 'Warned you what would happen.'

Lupin wheeled her mount, and tried to ride back down the trail. But the hired horse was a pudding foot and it gave her trouble. The lawman rammed his mount into hers, sent it staggering and whinnying and Lupin dismounted. Turgoose immediately swung around and lashed out with a boot. Lupin went down, the breath bursting from her as she rolled on to her side. Turgoose climbed down from the saddle and pulled her back to her feet, smacked her about the head with the flat of his hand as she tried to protect her face. He punched her brutally in the stomach and she gagged, bent double. He flung her to the ground again, where she lay, knees drawn up protectively as she tried to regain her breath.

'Just had to get smart, didn't you?' he panted. 'I know it was you turned Jesse loose, an' you know where he's gone to hidin'.' The man held his fists at his sides, opened and closed them with a mixture of excitement and anger. 'I figured to follow you. I knew you'd lead me to him, but I found enough of his tracks to know he didn't come *this* way,' he went on. 'Even if he doubled back this mornin', he couldn't get over here without someone seein' him. You didn't think of that, did you?'

Turgoose prodded her again with his boot, and Lupin edged away in fear of another kick.

'You been leadin' me blind, but that ends right now,' he threatened. 'You start tellin' me what's what, or I'll see that brat o' yours is taken away. I'll bulldog him into some Lamplight orphanage. For good luck, I'll jug you for helpin' a prisoner to escape. How'd you like the sound o' that, grease ball?'

Turgoose knew he held the cards, and he gave a short, triumphant laugh. As for Lupin, she might not have broken under his rough handling, but at the first suggestion of any harm coming to her child, the fear broke out in her face.

'All right,' she breathed despairingly. 'It was me helped Jesse get out of jail.'

'Hell, I already know that,' Turgoose snorted. 'I want to know where he's at now.' He saw Lupin hesitate and he grinned again. 'You ain't got long. In a minute or two, I'm takin' you back to town. Then I'll see about buyin' a train ticket to El Paso.'

'I can take you to him,' Lupin offered, looking and sounding defeated. She recalled Jesse telling her that he'd see her coming, hoped they wouldn't take him by surprise.

'I ain't that stupid,' Turgoose responded, as if he'd guessed Lupin's thinking. 'Just tell me.'

But Lupin was very worried, had little alternative. 'I've got to show you. You won't find the place on your own.'

The sheriff nudged her roughly and her body arched in anticipation of more pain.

'You try anythin' . . . anythin' at all, an' you'll be kissin' this dirt for keeps. You hear me?' he rasped. Then he made another of his short, snorting laughs. 'I'm thinkin' that takin' you along, maybe ain't such a bad idea after all. Could be I'll need somethin' to haggle with,' he speculated. Then he pulled the big bandanna from his neck and prepared

183

to gag her, but paused.

'Ain't goin' to be much fun havin' my clammy ol' scarf stuffed into your cute little chops,' he said. 'So, I'm thinkin' you tell me what the burr is under Jesse's saddle, an' I'll go easy. What do you say?'

Lupin knew she had run out of choices, that right now, she couldn't do Jesse any more harm.

'Jesse thinks his brother cheated him over the Triple T,' she answered. 'I saw Owen and his father together on the trail above Buzzard Point . . . the day Mr Tripp died. That's all I know. Make of it what you will.'

The sheriff's eyes narrowed. 'Hmm, short an' sweet, but tasty for all that,' he said. 'I always kind o' suspected Owen knew more about the old man's death than he let on. Perhaps you *will* come in handy.'

Lupin shook her head unhappily, took a furtive look around her, desperately wanted Jesse to appear.

Turgoose was eyeing her thoughtfully. 'Tell me, why don't you use that eye an' ear witness stuff to get your kid taken care of? You could likely squeeze him for plenty.'

If only you knew, Lupin thought. Turgoose's scheme came as a surprise, nonetheless. She had never thought about blackmail, or seeking money any other way. 'Owen Tripp is Manolito's father. Perhaps *that's* why,' was her curt response.

Turgoose swore an oath of astonishment. 'Well perhaps he'd be willin' to cough up a thousand or two to make sure I don't have another look into his father's death,' he added. 'I could put out a summons . . . subpoena you as a witness. He'd pay up or lose everythin'.'

'I want nothing from Owen Tripp,' Lupin said.

Turgoose laughed unpleasantly. 'Well, that's the difference between you an' me, Mex. I want plenty.'

Lupin squirmed as he suddenly started to loop the bandanna around her.

'You said you wouldn't — ' she started protesting as Turgoose rammed his neck scarf tightly between her teeth and tied it behind her neck.

'You don't get to be sheriff by bein' honest,' he sneered and hauled her roughly to her feet. 'I say I won't be doin' lots o' stuff, but I do. Now you take us on to where Jesse is,' he commanded. 'First sign o' you tryin' to pull somethin', an' we're straight back to town. That's when you say goodbye to the little *mestizo*.'

20

Holly Tripp reined in her bay mare, stared up the Cottonwood creek as Jesse walked towards her.

'You come back to relive the past again?' he greeted her.

'Not quite, Jesse. I've brought you some supplies. Lupin was afraid the sheriff would follow her, so she's led him off somewhere else.'

'Good,' Jesse said. 'Here really ain't a safe place to be.' Then he took the reins and looked at the burlap-wrapped bundle she indicated behind her cantle. 'I understood you an' Lupin didn't see eye to eye,' he continued, with an uncertain grin. 'What's changed?'

Holly dismounted and Jesse took a step back. 'Me. I've learned somethin',' she started. Then, watching him closely, she told of how the night before she'd overheard Owen and Luke Bogan in her front parlour. 'I went to see Lupin, to ask her if Owen was the father. Of course she admitted it, but *you* knew all the time, didn't you, Jesse?'

Jesse gave a slight shrug. 'I guessed it. I knew who it wasn't.'

'How could you let me think it was *you* all this time?'

'You made up your own mind, Holly, like everyone else.' Jesse gave her a sober look, shook his head slowly.

Holly nodded. 'An' I suppose I deserve all I got.'

'That was the Triple T when you married Owen,' he said with a weak smile, and for a moment, thought she was going to strike back at him.

'There's an old saw about gain bein' temporary an' uncertain. Hell, ain't that the truth,' she countered, to Jesse's surprise.

'Well you've certainly paid a price. I'm not certain whether he meant to, or whether it was an accident, but I am certain Owen's responsible for Pa's death. Maybe you're married to a murderer,

Holly, an' I'm goin' to find out.'

'You're not goin' to the ranch?' Holly asked anxiously.

'Do you know a better way? Maybe put a question in the personal column of the *Gazette*?'

'But what do you gain? What does anyone gain? He'll deny it, so it won't prove anythin'.'

'It will when I get my hands on those documents,' Jesse said confidently. 'Anyway, I'm not so sure I want or need any proof. It's got more to do with me an' Owen.'

'But you need to know the facts o' your father's death?'

Jesse looked at Holly steadily. 'Oh yeah, I need to know that.' Then the trace of a smile broke. 'Thanks for comin' out here. What's in the bundle?' he asked.

Holly untied the bundle on some dried tomatoes, a slab of cheese, bread and some bacon rashers. They sat in the lee of the bay mare, and Jesse shook his head when she offered to make a fire

189

for coffee, As he was washing his hefty sandwich down with water, Holly placed a hand on his forearm.

'It seems I've made more than a few mistakes, Jesse. Perhaps I can try an' put one of 'em right,' she said.

'Cheese an' bacon's just fine, Holly. I ain't a greedy man.'

'I meant by tellin' you somethi',' she countered. 'I want you to know that it wasn't for money, or land, or any other worldly goods that I married Owen. I married him because I was jealous o' Lupin . . . mad at you.'

'That must be a cheerless thing, Holly. But somethin' tells me you'll come out of it all with few scars. Let's start by gettin' on to the house,' Jesse decided.

Jesse got to his feet and looked back to where the claybank was tethered. Then something else caught his eye and he froze and cursed vehemently. On the west side of the Cottonwood, John Turgoose had Lupin bound and gagged in the saddle of her hired mount. The lawman had the barrel of his old Dragoon Colt pressed tight into her side.

'Jesse. You an' Holly just start walkin' towards me,' Turgoose shouted. 'Stay away from that Colt, an' don't go trippin' over Bogan. I don't have to spell anythin' out, do I?' he said, and nodded towards Lupin with a jerk of his head.

Jesse did as Turgoose ordered, while Holly offered him a pale face of worry. Jesse kept his eyes alternating between the sheriff and Lupin. He could see her dark eyes moving above the gag, but he couldn't understand anything she might have been trying to convey. He walked to the edge of the creek, with Holly alongside him. She had now seen the body of Bogan, was standing so close, he could feel her body start to tremble.

'Walk to the middle,' the lawman said, and Jesse started forward until he stood almost knee-deep. 'You stay where you are,' he called to Holly. He kept his eyes fixed on Jesse as he drew back the hammer of his Colt. 'I've chased me down an armed, escaped murderer,' he said with a wily grin. 'Now all I got to decide's whether to take him dead or alive.'

'Yeah, I wondered why you didn't want my gun. But then, you know I didn't murder anyone. That's right, ain't it, Sheriff?' Jesse returned. 'Samwell was killed by Luke Bogan. He told me so, just before he died.'

'Yeah? An' I wonder how ol' Luke managed that?' Turgoose said. 'Looks like it was a sudden case o' lead poisonin', administered by you.'

'There weren't any *sudden* about it, Sheriff,' Jesse replied. 'He'd already tried once to bushwhack me. He was carryin' the wound I gave him when he ran from Samwell's office. But don't believe me. Take a look, or listen to what Holly's got to say.'

Turgoose frowned. 'That so, Mrs Tripp?' he asked.

Holly hesitated just briefly before answering. 'Yes, Sheriff. Last night, my husband . . . Owen, had one of our house girls tend to Bogan's wound. I heard him make a threat, say Bogan was to go hide in Chimney Point. He's also got copies of the original will an' the faked one.'

Turgoose pursed his lips, muttered some garbled feelings. 'Thing is, Jesse, to me you're best dead,' he asserted. 'But Owen . . . well, he's a different matter. The pretty Mex here, tells me she saw him with ol' Festus at the time he died. With what Mrs Tripp's just said, I reckon Owen would be mighty willin' to put across some gratitude. Know what I mean?'

'Yeah, I know what you mean, Sheriff. It's kind o' reassurin' to know you won't get away with it,' Jesse said. 'I'm just hopin' your stupidity don't stretch to killin' these two witnesses.'

Jesse saw a muscle twitch under Turgoose's eye, guessed the man would strike back wildly if he was goaded any further.

'Hah, we all know I need both these

prairie flowers,' Turgoose answered. 'Mrs Mex here's the one who can put Owen up on Buzzard Point. An' she ain't goin' to offer trouble, 'cause if she does, that kid o' hers gets to board the next train to Texas.'

Jesse turned to one side, spat disgustedly into the swirl of water. 'You really are a piece o' work, Turgoose,' he rasped. 'Lower'n any rattler's ass.'

Turgoose laughed meanly and he glanced at Holly. 'You're a witness too, ma'am. An' if I — '

Jesse knew he was getting his last chance. Turgoose was so interested in his planning that he kept his eyes on Holly as he spoke. It was a slim chance, but it was the only one Jesse was going to get. When Turgoose stopped talking, he'd pull the trigger of his Colt and kill him where he stood.

For the shortest, divergent moment, Jesse wondered where Turgoose got his variety of guns, then, in one very quick move he drew his own Colt. The snap

194

of his arm caught the sheriff's eye and the man responded with an oath. It was that hair's-breadth of hesitation that was the difference between him living and dying.

Jesse's Navy Colt crashed out just ahead of the lawman's. Turgoose flinched, reared up in the stirrups, then toppled across his horse's rump. He hit the ground hard, managed a vinegary snarl as he fought to bring his gun up for a second shot.

Jesse shifted his feet for a better footing in the creek bed before snapping two steady, final shots into the lawman. Turgoose's body jerked as the lead struck him, and his six-gun fell from his grasp. He rolled on to his back, kicked out lamely with one leg, then lay very still.

Holly ran into the creek and grabbed at Jesse as he turned back towards the bank. Lupin's eyes were bulging and her jaw was grinding frantically under the gag, but she managed to swing down from her horse. She too ran forward, and Holly quickly started to untie her gag.

'Have you been hit?' Lupin asked Jesse anxiously, as he unbound her wrists.

'No, not hit . . . he caught me close though. Ribs'll be a bit bruised up.'

The three were drained, were staring at each other breathless, when they heard the cheery snort of an unfamiliar horse. They all turned, looked up the rise to see Owen Tripp approaching with a Winchester resting across his saddle.

'One o' the men reported gunfire along the Cottonwood about half an hour ago,' he said. 'I wondered if it was Luke got himself into trouble. Seems I was right.'

'Yeah, right on both counts, Brother,' Jesse replied. 'We half expected you to turn up. As for your foreman, well, he ain't headed for any more trouble. But good man that he was, he confessed before he died . . . spoke about the fake will, an' an alibi for you, the day you killed our pa.'

'No,' Owen cut in forcefully. 'It was an accident. There was a snake an' his horse reared a' he got throwed. That's what happened.'

'But you left him lyin' out there,' Jesse accused.

Owen nodded miserably. 'Yeah, I did that. He was dead . . . dyin', and I didn't know what to do . . . nothin' I could do. I had to let the sheriff's search take its course . . . knew he'd be found.' Owen dismounted and walked towards his brother. 'I didn't figure you'd ever show up here again, Jesse,' he continued. 'I had Samwell fake that will, but I swear to you, I didn't tell Bogan to kill Pa.'

'That part's true, Jesse,' Holly contributed. 'I heard him say.'

'So you figure everythin's square?' Jesse asked Owen.

Owen moved closer, looked directly into Jesse's eyes. 'Not *everythin*', Jesse. But I guess I thought we could sort *somethin*' out.' With that, Owen tentatively thrust out his right hand. Jesse looked down, but made no attempt to take it.

'Oh, we can sort somethin' out, Brother,' he offered. 'Just one overdue bit o' family business that needs settlin' up.'

21

Jesse unbuckled his gunbelt and handed it to Lupin. Then he moved forward purposefully, cursed under his breath for the want of being in some other place, for returning.

Hardly a muscle moved in Jesse's face, as he went in. He lashed out very quickly with his right fist, and Owen's head snapped back like the hinge on a cow pen. The man's lips were splitting tight against his teeth, and when his shoulders, backside and heels hit the ground flat out, Jesse was on him.

Owen was badly shaken, but his arch instinct for survival worked. He half turned, flung an arm around Jesse's neck, and clung tight. Jesse's knuckles drove into the back of his brother's head, but Owen swung himself over. Face down, he rose to get on to all-fours, reached for another neck grip.

Jesse dodged him and threw all his weight forward. Owen collapsed into the attack and together they rolled over and over through the bluestem grass, both growling with searing anger. They were struggling for an advantage, clawing for each other as ferocious and ruthless as distraught grizzlies.

They managed to climb to their feet, stood toe to toe, shocking each other with their enraged punches. Blood was pouring from their mouths and noses as Owen snapped them into a clinch. They staggered from side to side, backwards and forwards before going down heavily, with Jesse underneath. Owen thrust his left forearm under Jesse's chin and with the fingers of his right hand pulled at his face. Jesse lifted a leg as high as he could with his heel against Owen. He kicked inward and thrust his boot back down sharply. With a bellow of pain Owen flung himself away, staggered to regain his balance. One leg of his range pants had been ripped open, and blood streamed from where Jesse's spur had torn its way through.

They quartered the ground as they fought, sometimes throwing punches, sometimes manoeuvring for a hand-hold. Their lungs began to labour and rasp, and they staggered in unbalanced circles. Eventually, the muscles in their arms lost control, and their legs dragged heavily.

Owen was strong, but he lacked the fervour and purpose of Jesse. Watching cautiously, Jesse knew that if the fight went on much longer, they'd both go down. But it would be the one who went down first who'd stay there.

Owen was slumping now, could hardly lift his fists. He fought only in futile, defensive spurts and, as if to prove it, he lowered his head and went forward in one last despairing attack. A lucky aimless blow flung Jesse across the bowl of the old willow, and thrashing even more wildly, Owen plunged forward to try and finish the fight.

But Jesse was still thinking and he ducked, twisting quickly to one side. Owen missed with his punch and rolled hard around the meat of the tree. Jesse grunted, eased himself back and settled for grabbing as much of Owen's dark hair and ears as he could. He drew his brother's head back and banged his face solidly against the ridges of crusty bark.

Owen's body gave out and he sank to the ground, his head falling to the shallow creekside water that curled close around the roots of the tree. Breathless, Jesse lost his balance, and he fell exhausted on top of his brother. For a short time, both men lay without stirring, then Jesse pushed himself away. But he stopped when he noticed Owen's battered face was under the water, crushing against the bed pebbles. He gripped the damp jacket around the man's shoulders, and exerting his remaining strength, dragged his brother's upper body clear of the water.

'Pa woulda given you a fat ear for

comin' home after a scrap like this,' he said, 'An' you've got your feet wet.' He looked down at Owen's swollen, bruised face. But he was too weary for much brotherly sentiment, and regaining his footing, he wiped his face with his wet hands, leaned down and offered his hand for a pull up.

'I want half o' the Triple T, an' I want it in cash,' he stipulated sharply. 'Enough to get me the hell of a long ways from here.'

Holly helped Owen on to the bank and the sodden, beaten rancher gasped tiredly. 'I don't have that kind o' money,' he claimed with a chesty splutter.

'You will after roundup, an' the herd's sold,' Jesse said. 'We'll get a land agent in to value it. Should be worth a small fortune with all that extra land you've grabbed.'

Owen pushed Holly away in annoyance. 'You ain't owed any o' that. Pa left you a share in Triple T as it was when he died. What I added since then's mine.'

Jesse smiled thinly. 'You'd skin a flea for its hide, you would, Owen,' he answered back. 'I should've guessed a whuppin' from me weren't goin' to change anythi'. So it's the value when Pa died, then. That should be enough for us.'

'An' Holly's a witness to it,' Owen said.

Holly was now glaring at Jesse. 'Who's *us?*' she asked.

'Me an' Lupin.' Jesse considered saying he'd at least get something of Owen's to ride off with, but didn't think it would hurt enough.

Lupin watched the colour drain from Holly's face, and then she looked at Owen. He was getting to his feet, was thinking about how much a settlement would be. Then she took a long, deep breath and smiled.

Jesse was already walking away up the long grassy slope. 'I'd stay away from this place for a while. It ain't safe,' he called out. 'I'll let you know where to wire the money.'

We do hope that you have enjoyed reading this large print book.

Did you know that all of our titles are available for purchase?

We publish a wide range of high quality large print books including:
Romances, Mysteries, Classics
General Fiction
Non Fiction and Westerns

Special interest titles available in large print are:
The Little Oxford Dictionary
Music Book, Song Book
Hymn Book, Service Book

Also available from us courtesy of Oxford University Press:
Young Readers' Dictionary
(large print edition)
Young Readers' Thesaurus
(large print edition)

For further information or a free brochure, please contact us at:
Ulverscroft Large Print Books Ltd.,
The Green, Bradgate Road, Anstey,
Leicester, LE7 7FU, England.
Tel: (00 44) **0116 236 4325**
Fax: (00 44) **0116 234 0205**

Rafe and Seth Laramie were just trying to go home, but, mistakenly targeted by an angry posse, they are forced to flee a hail of bullets and hide out in the town of Greybull. There, the enigmatic Mort Sangster helps them to evade the posse. But all is not as it seems. The brothers follow Sangster to his cabin where outlaws, plotting an elaborate crime, invite them into the fold . . . but what bloody battles lie ahead if they accept?

THE TANGLEWOOD DESPERADOES

Logan Winters

Once you entered Tanglewood, in Southern Colorado, you could never find your way out. A savage, broken landscape — it was the perfect place to hide from the law. No lawman ever entered it, preferring the Tanglewood to do his work for him. So when Trace Dawson and his gang rode in, they were men without hope. Crooked land-pirates had taken their land and their homes from them. Now they were planning to fight back, whatever that might involve . . .

SCAR COUNTY SHOWDOWN

Elliot Long

When town marshal Arthur Curry is gunned down from behind by killers unknown, his brother, Sam, comes to Columbus to pay his last respects and to seek vengeance. The mayor, an old friend of Sam's, believes he knows who is responsible for the murderous crime. But Sam makes his own investigations, which lead him headfirst into a nightmare to which there is no easy solution. Time is ticking and there is a target on Sam's back . . .

THE SNAKE RIVER BOUNTY

Bill Shields

As a young man, Ben Hollinger hunted down and killed the outlaw gang who murdered his family. Now the marshal of a sleepy cattle town, he's forced into a gunfight with a young troublemaker, whom he kills — and his peace is shattered. Nate Thornton, the boy's father, owns the biggest ranch in the territory. The bounty he puts on Ben's head draws every local gun-hand to hunt him down. His only hope of survival lies with Cordelia — Thornton's daughter . . .

AMBUSH AT LAKOTA CROSSING

Terrell L. Bowers

Two old codgers manned Lakota Crossing; fifty miles from the nearest town. The perfect place for an ambush. Wayland Lott and his gang of killers were about to rob an army payroll at its way station, unaware that a bounty hunter was now working at the stage stop at Lakota Crossing. Jess Logan was pleased to finish out the winter there. But when the bandit gang began warring, the bounty hunter jumped straight into action — regardless of the consequences . . .